ON THE BANKS OF RIVER SARAYU

UNTOLD STORIES OF THE WOMEN OF INDIA

ON THE BANKS OF RIVER SARAYU

UNTOLD STORIES OF THE WOMEN OF INDIA

BHARATI SEN

Illustrations by Indrani Roy

G

Goldminds Publishing | St. Louis, MO

G

Goldminds Publishing
an imprint of Amphorae Publishing Group
St. Louis, MO 63116
Copyright © 2019 Bharati Sen
All rights reserved.

For information, contact info@amphoraepublishing.com

Manufactured in the United States of America
Set in Adobe Caslon Pro and Celestia Antiqua
Cover Design by Kristina Blank Makansi
Cover Art: Shutterstock / IStock
Library of Congress Control Number: 2019946593
ISBN: 9781946504487

I dedicate this book to my family,
to my enduring husband Amarjit,
to my wonderful two sons Shawn and Jay,
to my beautiful daughter-in-law Ruchy,
and to my gentle giant Gabriel,
I love you all.

And in loving memory of my parents
who always taught me about the importance
of giving back and helping those less fortunate.

CONTENTS

FOREWORD

KOLKATA IS THE CAPITAL of India's West Bengal state, and is nicknamed *The City of Joy*. Contrary to its name, it is a city of paradoxes. Still it seems to be the favored setting of my fictional stories, as I have lived a good part of my life in the big city. These stories provide fascinating glimpses into the panorama of baffling variety, its rich contrast of the simple and the sophisticated, the ancient and the modern. The characters are mostly drawn from women of Kolkata, focusing on the challenges of being a woman in India in a broader perspective.

While Indian media project women as outspoken, independent, and deeply conscious of individuality, the reality is quite the opposite. There are undercurrents and painful issues that still exist within the structure of the society, stories of exploitation of women and the imbalance in male-female relationships. What has changed is the consciousness and awareness that the existing imbalance should be removed by bringing out these problems into public view. And one cannot solve the problems unless one acknowledges that they exist even today.

The lives of the obscure, forgotten people who belong to the lower strata of society make me feel uncomfortable and empathetic when I visit Kolkata. The raging disparity and poverty-stricken faces still haunt me. These stories are about the people who made the streets of Kolkata their home – the unfortunate life of a rickshaw-puller's daughter, the plight of a washer man's wife, the lost dreams of a little maid, or the loveless life of a married woman. The characters in the stories are ordinary people one might encounter every day. They have themes and motifs of women's equality, struggles in marital relationships, and dilemmas attached to patriarchal traditions. They are ultimately about the living and breathing families in Kolkata of the past, and for some, even now in the present.

Through these stories, I hope to indulge readers about some of the traditional and socially accepted practices within Indian culture, some thoughtful and others potentially antiquated, but more importantly, relate to the emotional toll it levies on relationships and actions toward women in this particular society. The purpose of my writing is to express the troubles, woes, desires, inequality, and challenges that women in general experience. I want to share this world with my readers, knowing that by reading these stories, listening to their voice, may perhaps lead to improvement.

Many a time I have been told to write *happily ever after* stories. After all, we all enjoy the feeling of a fairytale ending. But it would be a blatant dishonesty to describe the real occurrences that are happening in real life each day, and so many times we easily turn our heads the other way. The reality of it all is that life is just as full of sadness as it is of happiness – it's bittersweet. To deny such a universal truth is to limit one's ability to write truthfully. These stories hope to convey that simple truth.

—Bharati Sen

NINETY

EVERYBODY KNEW HIM as Ninety's father, and he got so used to his surrogate name that he himself would introduce himself as Ninety's father. A familiar figure in town, people knew him in the markets, and the shopkeepers greeted him every time he passed by. They would even go to the extent of offering him tidbits and different kinds of sweets out of compassion. With eyes full of gratitude, he would bundle them up neatly in the big piece of cloth that he carried in his pocket and take them home to his beloved daughter.

Bishnu was his real name, named after Lord Vishnu, the Preserver of the Universe. He was far from being young and healthy as his long unkempt salt and pepper hair turned him into a scruffy, sluggardly old man. At times, he seemed to be spiritless, completely disregarding his ragged appearance, but he had a friendly smile that brightened his face.

He loved his daughter a little too much, favoring her over her older brothers. This was not appropriate because Ninety was the youngest in the family. For Bishnu, the happiness and well-being of his daughter was the first and foremost priority in his entire life. He would pick the best fish for Ninety from the fish market, and his face would light up whenever he visualized his daughter's reaction seeing a large piece of *rohu* fish on her plate. It was a delicacy for her. He was ready to make small sacrifices and refrained from buying other essential commodities that were on the list that his wife had been waiting eagerly for just so he could pick out the best fish for Ninety. The fishmongers were aware of his weakness and called out to him eagerly.

"Oh, Ninety's father, we have large pieces of fresh fish, straight from the river, take 250 grams of *pabda* and *rohu* for Ninety. We'll charge you less."

Bishnu grinned at their eagerness, felt hard to resist them, came forward and made room in his jute bag, even ready to encounter Ninety's mother's disgruntled face for his excessive indulgence towards the daughter. Her older brothers too, remained passive and had given up competing for their father's affection.

"How's your little daughter, Ninety?" The shop owners invariably asked him as he hopped from one shop to the other. He would talk about her gleefully. In fact, the whole fish market knew about the major milestones of her life.

"Did you know my little daughter started walking today? Did you know she took her first steps at the end of nine months? I still can't believe it, she's going to be incredibly smart." He would announce to the rows of fishmongers at the market who seemed to be taking pride in her little accomplishments.

"That's amazing, soon you'll be chasing her around the house," commented the guy who sat with a mound of small shrimps in the corner of the market, and there was laughter everywhere.

"Did you know she understands '*no*' and '*bye bye*'? She even spits out few words, '*Mama*' and '*Baba*' while she babbles and coos," Ninety's father would continue telling stories of Ninety quickly losing track of time.

One morning, fish sellers at the market were a little bit concerned at not seeing their regular customer. They wondered what could have happened to Bishnu. He did not come to buy fish. The next day, Ninety's father showed up to the market with worry and grief in his voice.

"I had to take Ninety to the hospital," he said. "She slipped in the kitchen and hit her head on the floor. I know accidents will always happen, but I was nervous to see bruises on her forehead and blood coming down from my baby's nose. I had to rush to the hospital to have a doctor see her."

"That's terrible, poor little Ninety! We were right when we thought something must have happened to her and that's why we didn't see you yesterday. Why don't you take this big piece of *chital* fish for her? It has less bones, so she'll love it," said one of the fishermen named Modhu enthusiastically. He had made a name for himself amongst his customers for being amiable and honest. He took hold of the jute bag and slipped two pieces of fish into the bag.

Bishnu's face lit up with his genial smile, the smile that earned him respect and endeared him to people who came to know him.

"But I want to pay for the fish, Modhu," He said.

"No," Modhu answered. "This is nothing compared to what you've done for me and my family. I'm deeply indebted to you for the rest of my life. How can I forget the night when my little son was sick, lying in bed with a high fever? I had no money to take him to the doctor or to buy medicines. You saved me by offering me money when I didn't have a job. You loaned me money to start my business in the fish market."

Bishnu smiled again and answered, "No, you don't have to mention it again and again Modhu, I didn't do anything out of the way. Anyone would've helped you; you don't owe me anything."

Why Bishnu named his daughter Ninety was a great mystery. Perhaps he came up with such an unusual name to make her special. It was her nickname and she did not have a proper name. His family, especially his wife, thought it unwise to name a girl child with such a preposterous name. In addition, Ninety was not aware of the fact that her name would be a provocation of amusement and laughter amongst her friends later on in life. In school, whenever the number ninety came up in math class, her friends started giggling. Some days she came home exasperated, urged her parents to change her name to a sweeter, more feminine name befitting a girl.

"I don't like my name, my friends always make fun of my name, why couldn't you find a better name for me?" She would say.

"Why can't you tell me why you call me Ninety," she asked her father directly. She asked her brothers, but they did not know. Her parents paid no heed to her remonstrations, it was not worthwhile to change the name at that age they said, when friends and families were quite at home with her being called Ninety. When she grew up, she eventually had no choice but to accept her name and cared less for the embarrassment her name solicited.

Ninety's mother, on the other hand, had developed a very different feeling towards her daughter. Far from having a mother-daughter special relationship, she was reluctant to look at her in the same loving way as her husband did. It was the fear of every mother that surrounded the birth of a daughter, and that was that they would not be able to find a husband for her.

She began to train her in household chores, encouraged Ninety to cook for the family, and always be obedient and respectful towards everyone. To her, those were the qualities every bride should carry before leaving for her in-law's house. From the day Ninety was born, her one absorbing thought was how to send Ninety off to an in-law's house. She began to anticipate the worst possibilities of not being married off at the right time and was extremely fearful of the possibility of her living the life of an unmarried girl. She would be the subject of gossip and ridicule.

At the same time, Ninety's mother was also aware of the unknown possibilities of rejection that her daughter might have to face. Like many mothers, she had a preconceived notion that sending girls to the in-law's house was like dropping them off at the door of Yama, the God of Death. She was aware of their hostility and the denigration the brides endure when they meet their husband's families.

Her daughter was not blessed with fair-colored skin, a negative point to solicit a good proposal. She wished Ninety had at least attractive features to add to her attributes. She was not well-educated and was not equipped with any skillful training that would allow her to be independent. But those who took the time to know her, would find she was a soft-spoken, good-natured girl.

Ninety learned to fast on Mondays, a rigorous fasting when she even refrained from drinking water. Mondays were auspicious days to worship Lord Shiva, and she would go to the temple to pray and pour coconut water on Shiva's head as a symbol of pacification. After all, Lord Shiva was believed to have the ultimate power of changing her destiny. Her sole desire was to please him with her rigid observance of fasts because a husband like Shiva was what she asked for.

Realizing that her parents worried about finding a match for her, she began to have sleepless nights. Some nights she would be awakened by the sound of voices in the adjoining room and, through the walls, she could hear her parents arguing about her. It was always her mother who would start.

"Shuncho?" (*Are you listening?*) She would start the conversation. Because she was respectful towards her husband, as customary, she did not address him by his first name. "Did you put a blindfold on your eyes?"

"What do you mean?" Her husband answered as he got into bed.

"It's about your precious daughter. She is no longer your little girl anymore. How long will you keep her on your lap? You need to find a husband for her. You know a lot of people in the market. Drop a hint here and there. There must be a suitable match for Ninety."

"What can I do? I have tried to find a suitable groom for her." He paused. "Think about Ninety too. She has been rejected seven times by grooms' parents. Every time she was refused, she would lock herself in her room and cry herself to sleep. Please don't give up on her so easily. Someday, somebody will surely like her." Bishnu, half asleep now, turned on his side. "When time comes, she will definitely get married, don't worry so much."

Besides finding a match for their daughter, they had one predicament that was eating away at them. It was the procurement of dowry money. It was almost certain a groom's side would demand an exorbitant amount for their daughter.

Eventually, Ninety's mother came up with a novel idea. Ninety had three older brothers. They were eligible enough to get married and ask for dowry money themselves, enough to cover Ninety's wedding expenses.

Her hopes and dreams of collecting dowry from her daughters-in-law were fulfilled in no time. Soon, two out of her three sons got married. Though they were not in favor of asking for dowries, but they did relent at their mother's insistence. The brothers, too, wanted to have a decent wedding for their only sister whom they loved dearly.

The older son brought in a huge sum of cash in the form of dowry. He was educated and had a decent job. Ninety's mother became a little more ambitious in her demands regarding her son's dowry. She wanted more material things.

"Don't you think the new bride would want to drink cold water, why didn't you ask for a refrigerator from the girl's family? A car would have been nice too, we could bring Ninety's groom in the car." She suggested.

Two years later the second son got married. He was not as marketable as his older brother, but he ended up marrying a bride who was the only child. So, dowry in the form of hard cash started pouring in. Gold ornaments weighing about 50 tolas brought a smile to Ninety's mother's face. She envisioned Ninety wearing every one of the gold jewelries that her second daughter-in-law brought.

Worries escalated when Ninety turned twenty-two years old. The midnight conversations and hushed arguments became frequent, laden with both hopes and despair. They were ready with all the money and jewelries that they needed to see their daughter off, but there was no groom.

Meanwhile, a few blocks away from where they lived, on the same street lived the Saha family. The family had a set of a brother and a sister whose parents were equally in a lot of strain of finding a perfect match for their children.

The door seemed to open for Ninety. As it was planned, the Saha family was invited for dinner at the house of Ninety's parents. The two families came to know each other; eventually they became good friends preliminary to the broaching of marriage proposals.

They asked for Saha's daughter's hand in marriage for their third son, but laid out a condition before them. Ninety's parents promised to refrain from taking any dowry for their son only if Saha's son married Ninety. It was an arrangement to which both sets of parents agreed without giving much thought.

In due time Ninety married her brother's brother-in-law. From its inception, however, the matrimonial alliance showed signs of weakness. The Saha's felt that they were tricked into having to marry their son to Ninety, who was lacking in expectations they had been looking in a bride.

Ninety on her part did all that she could to please her newly married husband and his family, but her life was a life full of insults and humiliations from the moment she entered their home. At first, her husband chose to stay aloof and did not concede to the adverse feelings of his family towards his wife. Nevertheless, he too became a victim to their persistent ill treatment. He slowly turned his mind against his wife. Had there been something in her possession she would have worked hard to make her husband turn towards her, but she had nothing to offer to make him love her and fight for her.

Once in a while, Bishnu would visit his daughter. He, too, noticed that the marriage wasn't quite blissful. Ninety tried hard to conceal her unfavorable state of affairs. When she saw her father, she pretended as if everything was fine. But her father did not fail to see her frail form and her lonely face. He knew his daughter was not happy.

In the meantime, Ninety lost her mother. It was a sudden illness that precipitated her early demise. Knowing her father was all by himself since her brothers and their wives did not live at home, Ninety asked her in-laws for permission to stay with her father during his bereavement.

It was like old days. Ninety took care of her father, shared chores that they both enjoyed doing. Bishnu, too, was happy to have his daughter by his side. Without his wife, he became more dependent on her. Ultimately, however, when it came time to go back to her husband, Ninety began to have doubts and trepidations. Bishnu convinced her that she must go back and that was where she belonged.

He accompanied Ninety to where the Saha's lived, and they waited anxiously at the door but were not allowed in. The old man was told to take back his daughter and that they had no need of her. With a heavy sigh, Bishnu sat down at the threshold of the door asking his son-in-law earnestly to take his wife back. Ninety took her father's hands in her own and asked him to stand up. There were no tears in her eyes, but a faint expression of relief on her face as father and daughter walked on to the streets.

Four years passed by, and Ninety and her father lived in the same old house. They shared daily chores and enjoyed each other's company. Bishnu had now given up on finding suitors for his beloved daughter. They both accepted the fate, living peacefully and contently.

One late afternoon near sunset, the two of them made a trip to the market, when a familiar voice from behind called out to Bishnu.

"Oh, Ninety's father!"

Bishnu turned and saw the face of one of the fishermen from which he would buy Rohu fish. It was Modhu.

"Is this your daughter, Ninety?"

Bishnu, at first hesitant to answer, nodded and then reached out and held Ninety's hand, anticipating some form of ridiculing.

"She's very beautiful." The fisherman replied with a warm smile. "You know," looking toward Ninety, "over the years, you have been a big reason for the success of my business."

Ninety began blushing and experienced the unfamiliar feeling of a compliment. A young man in a simple white t-shirt came out of the back of the store with a large basket of fresh *Rohu* fish. He stopped and smiled at Ninety.

The fisherman noticed the two of them and grinned. "What would you say about a marriage proposal for my son and your daughter?"

Bishnu was speechless. A rush of emotions mixed with thoughts flooding his head resulted in a frozen expression.

After a moment, Bishnu replied, "I don't know what to say, we have very little money now and cannot afford to give you a large dowry."

The fisherman stopped smiling. His face began to look scornful. His hands crossed as he grabbed his chin stroking his mustache pensively. "Well, I'm afraid I will require a dowry," the fisherman said reluctantly. Bishnu knew this was too good to be true and began to compose his usual forsaken expression.

"I will require ninety cents! Along with her happiness," continued the fisherman as his smile resumed and he opened his arms signaling Ninety to come to him.

Bishnu could not help but cry as he saw the fisherman embrace Ninety in the same fashion he had cared for her all her life.

Ninety finally smiled and introduced herself to the fisherman's son. Shyly, she asked, "What is your name?"

In a warm voice, the young man replied, "My name is Shivam."

THE NECKLACE

TO BUY CUSTOM-MADE pieces of jewelry in Kolkata, one must make a trip to *Bow Bazaar* Street in Central Kolkata, renamed as *Bepin Behari Ganguly* Street. Walking westward from Sealdah Railway Station on this street, it is hard to miss the presence of jewelry shops in the narrow alleys of Bow Bazaar market. It is still known as Kolkata's jewelry district, where every shop holds a variety of handmade gold and silver ornaments crafted in exquisite designs of heirloom quality, each curl and flourish telling a tale of heritage and of a culture that once was.

There are shops with a number of goldsmiths to cater to the customers, each of them working independently on their own designs. Typically, hunched over an old wooden table, with a face deep in concentration, he creates ornaments made to order from intricate designs either offered by him or as suggested by the customer. The basic tools of the trade are his trusty hammer, drill files, screws, a blowpipe, sandpaper, water and a stove. Using a burner, he melts gold, pours it into a mold, brings it to a desired shape and cuts it into a design before giving it a final polish. A goldsmith is required to be good at drawing the designs, important for creating gemstone jewelry. During wedding season and major festivals, orders come pouring in making it an extremely busy time of the year with often very long days of work in the shop. Sometimes a goldsmith is even required to go to a customer's house either to take the order or deliver the ornaments.

Mahesh and Jogesh Das, two brothers, owned one such shop in the jewelry district. Since all the shops sold different designs, it benefited the customers to walk into various shops and compare the products and their relative prices commensurate to their satisfaction. The *Das Brothers Jewelers* stood at the corner of the street and there was hardly a chance of missing it.

Mahesh, the older brother, who was a man of higher abilities, handled the management, while his younger brother, Jogesh, was the actual artist, the goldsmith who knew the trade. The shop consisted of a casting room where Jogesh would spend hours polishing, stone setting, repairing and soldering jewelries.

Jogesh's little daughter, Krishnakoli, sometimes sat on the steps of the shop in her leisure hours waiting expectantly and in anticipation of the passersby to come into the shop. She would carry a bowl of puffed rice on her lap and scoop handfuls into her mouth every now and then. It seemed as if she was always at the beck and call of her family, scurrying back into the inner quarters of the house in haste to fulfill one task or another that was entrusted upon her tender shoulders.

Jogesh and Sarala, her mother, were always obliging and trying hard to be on amicable terms with the older brother and his wife. Although Jogesh had the skills of a goldsmith, he was relegated to an inferior position in the house. Mahesh on the other hand, was a man of strong personality, and hence the master of the house. Since Mahesh managed the business, the major part of the profit from the shop went to him. The younger brother had a deep sense of respect for his older brother and avoided unpleasant confrontations with him in any matter, let alone money. They almost never ended well for him.

One morning, Sarala stepped into her daughter's bedroom with a small stainless-steel bowl in her hand.

"Krishnakoli, wake up! I ground turmeric paste for you, get up quickly and apply it on your face and body before it gets dried; come on now."

This was one of Sarala's many chores. Every morning she would grind raw turmeric into a fine paste using mortar and pestle, which she then mixed with gram flour and yogurt to turn the mixture into a viscous and redolent facial scrub. At her mother's continuous bickering and insistence, the little girl would apply the paste on herself everyday with much reluctance, amidst mockery and sarcasm from other members of the family. It was a constant reminder that she was not an attractive girl at all and that she had little to almost no hope of landing a decent proposal or a marriage alliance.

"How on earth would you find a groom for Krishnakoli?"

Mahesh's wife taunted her often, "As if dabbing turmeric paste on herself will turn her into a bespoke beauty overnight, you might as well look for other remedies to brighten up her skin."

The remark splashed cold water on Sarala's efforts and belief that her daughter would in fact be a fair skinned, hence lovely girl, one day.

Mahesh's wife had a mouth; her words took force from the fact that her daughter Oly was of fair complexion. Sarala found this reality hard to accept. To counter her daughter's not so bright marriage prospects, Sarala began to look at other natural remedies for lightening Krishnakoli's complexion.

"Rub fresh lemon juice and leave it on the skin for ten minutes," her neighbor Kutti advised.

One morning Kutti came in with a beaming face and said, "I prepared a face pack for Krishnakoli, a perfect choice for skin lightening, a paste made with tomatoes and gram flour!"

Aside from the concoctions Sarala made for her daughter using tender coconut water, yogurt packs were also applied every evening on her. Pieces of papaya were shoved into Krishnakoli's mouth every morning to exfoliate her skin. Some days her mother even gave her hot oil massages, all for the sole, elusive ambition of having a fair-skinned daughter.

Jogesh, on the other hand, was rather unperturbed by the shadowy quality of his daughter's complexion. Ever since she was a child, he sang to her only one song,

Krishnakoli I have named her, even though she was dark, on a cloudy day I did see the dark lass on a stretch of green, her doe eyes so deep and dusky. I had seen her long tresses tumbled down her back.

He hummed these words into her ears just to let her know that even though she was not a fair girl she had other attributes, like her doe eyes and her beautiful dark hair, as Bengal's poet laureate Rabindranath Tagore famously sang of his ebony love.

Oly, Mahesh's daughter, on the other hand, was fortunately not subjected to this daily routine for she was naturally light-skinned. Her parents had heaved an audible sigh of relief upon seeing their baby girl in the arms of the nurse. Maybe her dowry price would not be as high as others' since she was so fair. It was a fact that a dark-complexioned girl could still be married off if the parents provided a huge dowry for their daughter.

Mahesh and his wife took extra care of Oly, so that her skin color was maintained. She was forbidden from going out in the sun lest her skin tanned and was confined indoors while children of the neighborhood clamored day and night outside playing.

Unlike her cousin Krishnakoli, Oly used products that were found on shelves, creams like *Fair and Lovely*, a brand of whitening cream that was available in the market.

When Oly turned eighteen, her parents lost no time looking for a perfect match for their daughter. Since she was so attractive, Oly's marriage proposals started to pour in much like the way bees would rush to a fragrant flower.

Krishnakoli, a year younger than her cousin, bloomed into a pleasant looking youthful girl too. But she shied away from the thought of getting married early and concentrated on her studies instead. She wanted to get a job to help her father with the dowry money for the future.

In the meantime, Jogesh, had been saving scraps of gold in order to make a bridal *necklace* for Krishnakoli one day. After a year or so, he put a red velvet box stealthily into his wife's hand.

"Keep it in a safe and secure place. I worked day and night putting finishing touches to this bridal necklace for Krishnakoli. I want to surprise her with it. That is the only piece of jewelry she is getting from us, and I put my heart and soul into making it," he told her in a hushed tone. He paused for a moment, "When Krishnakoli has a daughter of her own, only then, should she pass it on when it is time for her daughter to get married."

Sarala opened to see what it was. Inside the box, lay a gold necklace. The enchanting *Navaratna* necklace had intricate filigree work in a traditional setting and an arrangement of nine gems. A ruby glowed in the center, surrounded by other natural stones: a diamond, a pearl, red coral, blue sapphire, cat's eye, a yellow sapphire and an emerald. These gems were known to have astrological powers to protect and also bring good luck to the wearer. However, they had the opposite effect too if it did not suit a person.

"When did you make this exquisite necklace, what an absolute beauty!" His wife exclaimed in absolute surprise. Sarala couldn't believe her eyes. She played with the necklace, placed it on her own neck to see the effect of it on herself. Jogesh turned over the jewelry to show her the letter "K" underneath, beautifully engraved and personalized. Krishnakoli would be wearing it on her wedding day. The red velvet box was concealed, wrapped inside an old shawl securely. She looked around to see if anybody was watching her and then deposited it inside an old trunk with a broken latch.

Indian tradition requires a bride's family to provide her with a certain amount of gold jewelry, an item of value and is also part of her dowry. As a result, top priority was always given to the procurement of gold jewelry for prospective brides, wherein her worth would be determined by the amount of gold she brought as her wedding dowry.

For Oly, her parents amassed a sizable amount of gold over the years.

"She should look even prettier than the Goddess Lakshmi, I'm going to cover her from head to toe with gold," Mahesh remarked in every one's presence.

When she was twenty, Oly was married off to a suitable groom that her parents arranged. On the day of her wedding, she bedecked herself with all the gold that her parents had procured for her.

While getting ready for the wedding with Oly's mother, Sarala opened her broken suitcase to see what she could wear for the occasion. As she did so, one corner of the red velvet box came into view.

Before she had the chance to cover the box back with the shawl, Oly's mother grabbed it from her hand and her eyes sparkled at the sight of the gorgeous necklace.

"Where did you get this?" She barked.

"Where did you get all the money, where has it come from? You secretive woman, you kept it to yourself knowing that my daughter is getting married before your daughter. Here you are making jewelry for your own daughter without our knowledge. Mahesh should be told; he has to know what is happening with his store money."

Sarala's face fell, but she gathered herself quickly.

"Krishnakoli's father made it for her so that she will have something to wear on her wedding day."

She was not a person to give up her curiosity, so she asked Sarala where did Jogesh come into possession of so much gold.

Sarala told her how her husband had made the necklace from scraps of gold collected over the years.

"Then it rightfully belongs to Oly, as the scraps of gold came from the shop."

Mahesh's wife turned on her heels and walked off, the necklace swinging from her hand.

Soon, Jogesh's necklace found its place amidst the tiers of gold around Oly's neck on her wedding day.

At the wedding ceremony, Jogesh did not fail to notice his daughter's necklace on Oly's neck. He consoled his wife saying he would make another one for their daughter. After all, she was not going to get married soon.

After a while, Oly started wriggling in the midst of the prolonged wedding ceremony. She kept touching her neck and fidgeting with the necklace. The necklace seemed to bother her. It was not staying in place, and every time she made a move, the necklace pinched her. The long chain that she was wearing seemed to get entangled with the necklace, and gradually, the skin around her neck turned red and itchy. A feeling of uneasiness engulfed her. Before long, she decided to take it off and gave it back to her mother.

The next evening, when Oly was leaving for her in-law's house, her mother quietly tucked the red velvet box with the necklace inside, with her other jewelries.

It so happened that, as days went by, whenever Oly tried to put on the necklace, a strange feeling passed through her, almost suffocating her. She began to realize that the necklace did not make her feel quite right. She thought she would soon tell her mother to give the necklace back to Krishnakoli, but completely forgot about it.

In the meantime, Jogesh resumed piling scraps of gold to remake the lost necklace. It was a laborious job and took a toll on his health. Long periods of sitting still did not allow him to make any movement with his body. Back muscles, like any other muscle, require adequate exercise to maintain vigor. If they are immobile, they tend to weaken with age. He was soon diagnosed with fibromyalgia, characterized by widespread pain in tender points of muscles and joints, including the head, neck and sides of hips. In a short time he became so sick that he left the necklace unfinished.

In Oly's household, things were not falling into place either. Small mishaps, unaccountable losses in cash and kind, and health issues affected them. Twice their home was burglarized by thieves, and even their car was stolen. Oly's husband and her in-laws began to think that Oly had brought horrible bad luck upon the family, for the reason that all these unfortunate incidents were taking place with her arrival into the house. One morning, Oly surprised her parents when she appeared outside her father's door with a small suitcase containing what belongings she possessed. She had been kicked out of her husband's home. Both Mahesh and his wife failed to understand why their daughter was sent back without any plausible reason.

As she was organizing her belongings at her father's place, her jewelries readied to be stowed away in a safe and secure place, she opened the red velvet box that contained Krishnakoli's necklace. To her amazement, she found that the necklace had lost its original color, looked dull and lost its luster. Oly begged her mother to return it back to her aunt and explain how uncomfortable she felt every time she wore it.

"Why don't you give it back to Krishnakoli, it rightfully belongs to her. I have so much, and I don't really care for that piece of jewelry anymore. You've given me enough." Oly told her mother. Within days, the red velvet box found its way back into Sarala's hands. Jogesh also began showing signs of recovery. He was overjoyed to have the necklace back and polished it again and again until the necklace regained its former luminosity, becoming even brighter than before.

Krishnakoli's mother's concern for her daughter's complexion started to wear off as the years went by. The breakup of Oly's marriage had opened her eyes, showing that after all it was not the color of the skin that was going to save the marriage. It was the hands of the Divine Providence who had His own plans of making and remaking the destinies of people.

Krishnakoli was drawn into a life where marriage mattered little for her. She finished her studies and soon found a job that made her very happy. She did not have to rely on her parents and learned to make her own decisions. At work she befriended a colleague and one day, brought him home for her parent's approval.

Once again, the sounds of the marriage pipes and melodies of the shehnai sounded in the Das house, announcing Krishnakoli's impending wedding. She was pampered and had the attention of the entire household. Relatives came from distant places to attend her wedding. When she made her appearance, fully dressed up like a bride, Sarala put the necklace on her daughter's slender neck as a finishing touch. It brightened up her face with an extra glow from the reflections of the jewelry. Meanwhile, Oly's husband and his family came to the realization that they had been harsh towards their daughter-in-law and started working towards reconciliation.

When Krishnakoli came into possession of the necklace, it acted like a magic charm in her life. On every auspicious day, she wore the necklace and when life had its own adversities she turned to the necklace, touched it, put it around her neck to remove all obstacles in her life. She came out unscathed as if somebody was always watching out for her. She relied so much on the object that she almost became obsessed with it. She constantly feared that she might lose it one day or a burglar might steal it. There was something about the necklace that could not be explained. Contrary to what happened with Oly, the necklace had brought nothing but good luck to Krishnakoli throughout her life. However, she knew that one day the time would come to part with the necklace.

Years later, at the time of her own daughter Konkona's wedding, it was the custom and family tradition that she would have to hand the necklace over to the next in line and her daughter Konkona would be the new rightful owner. She soon began to worry about her own future and began to envisage a life without her necklace.

Am I not the rightful owner, I must keep it for my own benefits! She thought.

So Krishnakoli visited a goldsmith who could make an exact replica of the gold necklace. On her daughter's wedding day, she kept the original one and passed on the duplicate to her daughter without the knowledge of anyone in the family. However, it turned out to be an adverse decision and had a disastrous effect on her life. Her peaceful life crumbled right before her eyes and she had no power to control it. There were constant arguments between her and her husband, she was falling sick every now and then, they were financially depleted, her close friends did not want to be with her any more. Things began to fall apart in her life and she was shaken up furthermore when she was involved in a terrible accident that almost killed her and her husband.

Each time something terrible happened, she would run to her gold necklace for assurance by touching it, but the necklace came of no use and refused its magical charms for her. She rubbed it again and again as if it was a magical genie's lamp, but the necklace refused to show any trace of its former color. Suddenly, she thought of wearing it around her neck, as she did so, an uneasy choking sensation filled her up. Krishnakoli looked herself in the glass pane of her window and saw some redness on her neck. She then slowly unhooked the necklace and proceeded to store it in the red velvet box. She was full of remorse for not giving away the necklace to her own daughter. After all, she had it for a long time and enjoyed its magical touch, and she realized that it was her daughter's turn to keep the family heirloom. After a long sleepless night, she decided to tell Konkona the truth about the necklace. So the next day, Krishnakoli met her at her house carrying the original necklace with her.

"Listen to me, my dear," she said. "I hope you'll understand before I try to tell you what this is all about. You know about the beautiful necklace your grandfather made for me. In fact, everybody knows about the magical powers of the necklace. I have been clinging to it, solely because I thought I could not live without it, that my life depended on it. But I was wrong. I was supposed to hand it over to you, but instead I kept the real one and gave you a replica. Ever since that time, my life has been chaotic, full of misfortunes, as if there was war in every front. I can't handle it anymore. The realization came to me a few days ago when I turned to my necklace and saw that it had lost its luster. However hard I rubbed it, the necklace did not regain its original color."

During Diwali, the festival of the lights, Konkona could not wait to wear the beautiful necklace that her grandfather had created painstakingly.

"Mother, you've been right all along, the necklace had something to do with all the good things that are happening in our lives. It wraps around my neck as if it was meant for me, there is an added glow to my face whenever I put it on. Did I tell you that we made an offer on our new house?" She told her mother that day.

She came to realize that a part of her grandfather's life, his soul had remained in the necklace and that it had become a talisman representing protection and love.

"You look so elegant; it suits you perfectly." Krishnakoli gave an appreciative look at her daughter and then she added, "Before I forget, when you have a daughter or daughter-in-law of your own, pass it on, otherwise you will face many difficulties in your life. Always be grateful for what you possess and have in front of you, and remember that what we get, we should always be ready to give."

KONIKA THE MAID

A LOUD METALLIC CRASHING sound emitted suddenly, silencing all the other resonant domestic noises. It came from the kitchen of one of the apartments of Kailash Bhavan, a tall 10-story housing complex. Kitchen utensils, pots, and pans clattered on the marble floor reverberating through the thick walls of the residents. If one looked through the kitchen window of the Mazumdars, a little girl crouched on her knees would come into view. She was shocked into silence, solemn and puzzled, and gazed down at the mess she made, hurriedly picking up the utensils that accidentally fell from her small childish hands.

"Konika, you are so careless and distracted. Don't you see the dents you put on my stainless-steel cookware? These are expensive and part of my wedding trousseau.

My mother went to great lengths to collect them over the years and I can never replace them," Molina said angrily. "I want you to be more careful in the future. Next time anything happens like this I am going to deduct the damage from your salary."

Molina Mazumdar, the lady of the house whose outward appearance revealed all the comforts of life, was four times larger than the gaunt little girl servant. Konika knew that it was her fault and that she should have been more careful, so she did not say a word. She began to finger the dents as if she could smooth them back to their former shapes.

"Pick them up fast, I want you to go to Sadhana's grocery store and buy some mustard seeds; but come home soon and start making the mustard paste," Molina bellowed and snatched the dented pan from Konika. "For twenty-five grams of mustard seeds you probably need ten rupees, and bring back the change," she said.

Molina's neighbors claimed she was a good cook, but she had an irksome, annoying habit of buying spices in small quantities to replenish her pantry of ingredients she required daily. As a result, she was always low on the essential commodities. On top of that, she distrusted Konika with money and wanted to prevent Konika from stealing from her.

Konika enjoyed these little breaks to the market when she came into contact with the outside world, meeting other servant girls of different age groups from individual floors of the building. There was only one small grocery store across from the building, where all of the basic necessities were sold. The grocery store served another purpose, as it seemed to be the only place where these maids gossiped and exchanged their stories on the daily happenings in each of their respective households that they were employed. Konika in no time told her story of putting dents on her mistress's expensive pots and pans.

"Oh, you are lucky," said Pushpa, the girl with a dimple on her cheeks. "At least Molina Mashi did not hit you. If it were Shabita Mashi, she would not have spared you. Why just a few days back I broke one of her expensive teacups, and she pulled my hair and pushed me so hard that I hit the kitchen wall. The rolling pins become handy whenever she is angry, I still have some bumps on my head," she said.

Nirmala, the tall girl from apartment B/16 Kailash Bhavan, lifted her dress an inch above her knees to show a bruise that was partly healed.

"They always hit me whenever I do something wrong. I am not good at ironing clothes, and yesterday I put a burnt mark on the sari she told me to iron. Both husband and wife pounced on me."

Konika heard so many other stories and measured her fate to that of the others and concluded she was in a better position than Pushpa. At least she was spared the rod.

Konika came to work at the Mazumdar house when she was seven years old. Every day she would stand on the balcony and watch other girls of her own age go to school in their uniforms with book bags and small lunch boxes. Her mind wandered to their classrooms, teachers, and playgrounds, and she pondered what they could be carrying in their lunch boxes. Her mouth watered at the thought of all of the delicious snacks their mothers had prepared.

At Molina's house, Konika would get two handmade *rotis* with a very small amount of potato curry for dinner. Her lunch consisted of rice, lentils, and one vegetable item. It was the same food every day with no variations. There was always leftover food from the family, as lunch and dinner were cooked fresh each day, but only on rare occasions was Konika allowed to eat some of the leftovers. Konika was always hungry.

Sundays were special days when Molina made proper use of her culinary skills and prepared a savory mutton curry. The smell and preparation that went into making the goat meat would always make Konika's mouth water. She waited impatiently walking around the kitchen as the pressure cooker hissed and whistled. With every hiss, the aroma of the curry intensified and wafted in the air, filling the whole apartment building with the delicious smell of the prepared meat.

"Konika, go quickly," Molina said while handing her some rupees. "I need a small packet of turmeric powder, garlic, and ginger for the mutton curry."

When Konika returned, she laid out all the ingredients, and carefully made a paste of ginger and garlic, before washing and cutting the meat into small pieces. Normally when it was her time to eat, Konika did not see a single piece of meat on her plate, often only consuming the leftover liquid portion or *jhol*.

One Sunday afternoon, Konika decided to give herself away to her temptations. She knew if she wanted any of the mutton, she would need to get to it fast. When no one was watching, she pried the lid off the container, took in the aroma from the ginger and garlic paste, and made a desperate plunge into the dish, shoveling two mutton pieces into her mouth as if she were a contestant in a speed eating game. She dug her fingers into the gravy, picked up a meaty bone, and ate with haste scraping the last morsels of meat off the bone with her teeth. She wanted even more and became audacious as a result, willing to take on more risk. Over the weeks, Konika began to linger in the kitchen doing her chores leisurely on Sundays, and when noone was watching, she would quickly pop a sample of meat into her mouth.

One Sunday while opening the lid of the meat container, she felt a resounding whack on her back.

"How dare you, Konika, you little willful girl. You're eating away the whole pot of goat meat! You've contaminated it! How can I serve it to the rest of the family? Do you have any idea how much the meat costs?"

She was apprehended and was given no other food for the remainder of the day. For the next few weeks, Molina narrated the story of Konika's attempt to steal the goat meat to her friends and neighbors with many distortions and exaggerations so that others became watchful over their own servant girls.

As days progressed, Konika began showing streaks of early teenage rebellion much to the annoyance of Molina.

"Where is the girl now? I sent her to get some laundry detergent powder from the market and she has vanished!" Molina thought.

Thirty minutes later Konika showed up without the soap. Molina picked up the heap of dirty clothes and threw them at her.

"Where were you? I've been waiting for the detergent. Where is it?"

Konika kept quiet and continued rubbing her sticky hands on her dress.

"The ice cream vendor," she said in a muffled voice, looking down. "Pushpa and Nirmala were buying ice cream and I also bought some with the money you gave."

"I'm going to deduct that money from your salary, you greedy girl! Don't I feed you enough at home? You don't even get two meals at your father's house and here you are eating goat meat and what not! Don't just stand there and cry, go make a cup of tea for me! You've given me a headache. Wait until your father comes, I'll tell him what you did," Molina bellowed before her face turned back to a normal color from the reddish hue it previously fashioned.

Like every child, Konika woke up the next day with a fresh start. She tried to please Molina in every possible way, for she feared being sent back to her village where she would have to endure the abject poverty and miseries. She thought about her father's angry eyes and mother's disappointed face. Konika came from a peasant family and had three other siblings at home. Being a farmer, her father struggled to feed the growing family. Konika was the eldest and was quite capable of doing chores. So, when he came to the city, he prayed that his daughter would find a maidservant's job.

Konika's parents thought their daughter was far better off than other girls in the village. The fact that she had clothing provided by the family who hired her, the comfort of living in an air-conditioned apartment complex, and free meals every day sounded too good to be true. However, the fact of the matter was that her clothes were two sizes larger than her actual size and never fit her perfectly. Each outfit had some combination of buttons missing, colors that appeared faded, or seams that were coming out. They were mostly donated by the generous Aunties in the building whose daughters had outgrown these dresses. Konika looked forward to the acquisition of a new dress on one occasion each year during the *pujo* celebration of Goddess Ma Durga, a festival time when everyone was entitled to get a new dress. The thought of getting a new dress brightened up her little face, only to be diminished soon thereafter upon realizing her brothers and sisters at home were not as lucky as she was. Molina, who gave a plain, mustard-colored dress to Konika, was careful about deducting the cost of this new dress from her accumulated salary.

When all thoughts of happiness had faded, four years had passed, and a new family came to live in one of the apartments of Kailash Bhavan. A young man, his wife, and their baby girl were the only members of the family. The couple needed a helping hand for their baby. The young mother, named Bandana, had met Konika and thought she would be the perfect person to help her with her daughter. However, Bandana knew Konika was already employed, so to avoid any confrontation with Molina, Bandana cleverly waited for Konika's father, who would come visit once a month to collect Konika's salary, and approached him directly.

"I can offer twice the salary that Konika receives currently," Bandana offered.

Her father readily agreed without hesitation. For Konika, it was a wonderful stroke of good fortune. She not only found Bandana a kindhearted woman, but she also adored the baby. The prospect of playing with her filled her heart with happiness. However, when Molina found out, she did not spare Bandana from her venomous outbursts and hurled curses at her.

"How dare you steal my maidservant! I've trained her so well and now you took her away from me! I'm going to tell everybody in the building that you bribed her father," she barked at Bandana.

The next few years of Konika's life seemed to be peaceful and full of contentment. Bandana took good care of her as Konika did not have to steal food to get a good meal, nor did she have to worry about her clothing. Additionally, every year Konika was sent home to be with her family for a few days. Her parents were happy to see their daughter's turn of fate.

However, Bandana soon began to notice some changes in Konika. As a young adult, Konika became restless, and for the first time, began paying attention to her looks and appearance. Sometimes in exasperation Bandana called out to her: "Konika what's taking you so long in the bathroom? I want you to come with me to the fish market."

"Bandana Mashi, I'll be done in a minute."

But her minute quickly turned into an hour. When she finally appeared from the bathroom, Bandana's eyes did not fail to notice that Konika had put her long beautiful black hair into a tight braid, put powder on her face and a small red dot on her beautiful forehead. Originally walking barefoot when she first came from the village as a little girl, she now quickly wore slippers to cover her callused feet. She knew that going to the market could attract young lads who would potentially turn their heads when she passed them by.

"Is there someone in particular who you want to notice you?" asked Bandana, teasingly.

Konika's face quickly turned the same red color as her previous employer would turn when she would get scolded. She tucked her head down and smiled back.

When Konika turned seventeen, she befriended the young *darwan* (doorkeeper) of the apartment building. She would make excuses to go out of the house to spend several hours socializing with him. He would accompany her to the market and would continuously look up at the apartment complex windows, hoping that Konika would return a glance back.

"Konika seems to be absentminded nowadays. Her mind wanders far away. She no longer works like she previously did, and I am beginning to feel a bit concerned about her," Bandana confided her husband one day.

"Maybe she misses her family. How about if we call for her father to come to visit for a couple of days?" he said.

On the day Konika's father arrived, the young *darwan* thought it was an opportune time to ask his blessings in hopes to marry Konika. He attempted asking, however, having been brought up in a remote village relying on old traditions, Konika's father strictly forbid the union of the two after finding out that the *darwan* belonged to a low caste and had no social status. Even more disappointed with Konika who would even consider mingling with an untouchable, Konika's father irrationally decided to take her back to the village. Bandana regretted her decision to bring Konika's father to town, not knowing that it would result in Konika's departure.

Within a month of returning back to her own village, Konika's father consulted the horoscopes and found a match for Konika in the same caste with a fruit vendor from a neighboring village. He quickly agreed to the marriage and with a meager dowry, sent her to live with her new husband and family.

Despite what was thought to be a perfect match, Konika's story was far from a fairytale ending. Cruelties of mere existence pervaded once again into her life. The abuse began gradually, and her husband's need for controlling her made him subject her to false and meaningless accusations. She lived in fear and felt trapped in a violent relationship. When her body showed marks of cuts and bruises, she became reclusive to avoid the interference of her neighbors and friends. At the beginning of their relationship, her husband would quietly give Konika money to go to the market to buy essential ingredients in order to prepare a meal. But as things began changing, he would yell at her for wasting his money and have angry outbursts during every meal she prepared. Within six months of their relationship, he began coming home late at night, inebriated with the smell of cheap alcohol reeking from his breath. Regardless, Konika waited anxiously for her husband to come home, with his food served, neatly on a tin plate. She would always cover the food guarding it against nocturnal insects. She also never made a plate for herself and would wait for her husband to leave something for her to eat from his plate.

Matters escalated one day when her neighbor came to the door.

"Do you mind if I come inside, there's something I need to tell you," she told Konika. "I saw your husband with Lalitha last night, a woman of ill repute. He is with her tonight as well."

Konika's face remained flat until finally, her lower lip began to quiver. That was a final blow to her life, full of nothing but misery. To her dismay, she came to realize there was no way out for her. She could not go back to her father's house where she knew she would not be accepted. She quietly closed her eyes and imagined the warm smile of Bandana's company.

It was the monsoon months; constant rains prevented the fishermen of the village to venture out into the sea to procure fish. They bid their time for the rain to subside, and instead, stayed close to the shores to cast nets and catch the fish that lived in the shallow waters. Konika's husband too went to the shores netting some of those fresh fish in hopes to bring it home. When he came home that evening, he noticed his wife was not there waiting for him like every typical day. Evening rolled into night, but there was still no trace of Konika. She was nowhere to be found. Word spread amongst the villagers quickly who gathered together and went in search of her to nearby places the next day. They scanned the shores hoping they would find her, but after a while, the search was fruitless. On the fifth day of her disappearance, when the rain subsided, the larger fishing nets were hurled once again further out in the sea. One of the fishermen felt something heavy get caught in the net. When he pulled the net out of the water, he found a sari tangled with seaweed and dirt. Several villagers immediately recognized the sari was worn by Konika nearly every day when she would walk to the market. To much sorrow, the word was passed on to her husband that Konika had drowned herself to put an end to her misery.

Meanwhile, back in Kailash Bhavan, Bandana waited at the bus stop to see her little daughter off to school. A large white school bus arrived hastily, and in a similar manner, took off with a trail of black smoke toward its next destination. Bandana went back home, grabbed her purse and an empty bag, preparing to go to the market. Her thin maidservant joined her, and they walked quietly and peacefully to the market together. It was the time of Ma Durga festival once again, and Bandana loved wearing her blue sari with a set of keys tied in a knot at the end of her sari. The maidservant walked quietly beside her, while happily wearing a plain, mustard-colored dress.

DHOBI AND DHOBANI

A TYPICAL MORNING started for Raka. The doorbell rang announcing the arrival of the daily morning newspaper. The newspaper boy had stuck a newspaper in one of the grooves of her retractable collapsible gate. It had the typical smell of freshly printed pages of ink and paper as she held it in her hands. Raka gave a perfunctory glance at the headlines of the front page as she was more interested in the gossip columns on the back pages.

As she was about to turn the front page, her eyes caught a line that read, *A constitution for All India Washerman's Federation has been adopted due to the attempts of several leaders helping them form an organization. Thus, making it easier for the unification of different dhobi (washerman) associations.*

"It would be unwise for them to form a union," she thought to herself. "They should be satisfied with their lot, from now onwards the dhobis would engage themselves in petty grievances, call upon strikes and demand remunerations. Dukhiya had been so meek and gentle and he too will protest about every little thing!"

She heard the buzz of the doorbell ring for the second time. It was louder this time giving an impression that the ringer of the doorbell was in a rush.

"*I'll get it*!" She said as she hurried to the front door. She wrenched the door to open to let the sweeper come in to pick up the trash. He emptied the bin carefully and returned the container to be picked by the maid. The luxury of having too many household helpers was nice, but made Raka exhausted just with all of the helpers scurrying around in her apartment all the time.

Five minutes later, the doorbell of the front door buzzed louder than the previous ones, announcing its urgency. Through the collapsible gate, near the doorway, she could see the familiar shadow of a short, thick stocky man carrying a bundle of nicely stacked laundry in his large and sinewy hands. It was Dukhiya, the *dhobi*.

"Did you bring everything?" She asked.

Dukhiya smiled, "Yes, I brought all Memsaab", he said simply.

He opened his bundle and put the clothes on the couch, and immediately wiped off a huge drop of perspiration that hung from the tip of his nose. Routinely, he picked up a shirt to show Raka the code that he imprinted with black ink on the clothes of each household, as a mark of identification. It so happened that he would forget to bring one or two items or get mixed up with the identification of the clothes. He would then deliver them next day. Some clothes did not return at all, whether old or new. There always seemed to be a dispute, sometimes an argument between the dhobi and the lady of the house over the fact that Dukhiya did not keep an account of the clothes washed. He was mildly rebuked about his deplorable washing. Marks of stain, spots were not taken off properly, faint remnants could still be detected. The shirts wore out much sooner than usual, the cuffs were not mated, and the ring around the collar would remain the same. And often Raka's husband went to his office in a very bad humor. But the comfort of having the shirts that looked white and stiff made her overlook the considerable amount of loss of money over laundry.

"I did my best. If she did not like it, she could get someone else to do the washing," Dukhiya would say, whenever his feelings were hurt.

Raka opened the copybook to check the list of laundry. Slowly she began to sort out the crisp shirts, saris, trousers, all washed, starched and ironed, neatly folded.

She scrutinized every piece just to make sure if there was any tear, damage or any discoloration.

"Dukhiya, here's your money," she handed him some folded rupees.

He took the money with his gnarled, sinewy, dry hands, from a lifetime of scrubbing the clothes, touched it twice to his forehead before putting it in the huge pockets of his *kurta*, as he straightened the folds of his *dhoti*. He then swung his bundle over his shoulders and headed out for another house.

Raka called after him, "You make sure that your children do not go hungry, buy some vegetables from the market."

It so happened that Dukhiya, like all other *dhobis,* had a regular hangover from his daily intake of cheap alcohol. It could be bought easily from roadside small shops. And underneath those glassy eyes, there were revelations of sadness and utter resignation.

"Oh, all dhobis drink while they wash clothes," he would respond to Raka's concerns, trying to justfy his habit.

It was the *dhobani (washer woman), who was Dukhiya's wife,* that Raka cared about the most. She would not engage herself in any kind of dissention with her, regarding laundry. On the other hand, she tried to overlook her inefficiencies. Being a *dhobani*, she had no choice but to offer her help in the traditional occupation of washing clothes. There was no escape from this tedious job, no other line of work to turn her life around.

Elbows in dirty water, hands hard and wrinkled, the *dhobani* thought ruefully, "this is what my mother did and that's what her mother's mother did, and that's what I will do."

It was her task to carry laundry to and from households in the apartment complexes of the urban neighborhood. She would take away the dirty ones, and bring back the clean ones, neatly folded. Even her children were motivated to contribute their hours or work, one way or another. Some days the *dhobani* draped herself in a sari that someone else gave it for cleaning; she made good use of it before it went for cleaning. This was the norm.

From dawn till nightfall, the dhobi and his family washed clothes in rows of concrete wash pans where the clothes were soaked in sudsy water. Each item of clothing was washed with a flogging stone, and then thrashed violently against a nearby rock or at by the *ghat (staircase leading to a river or stream)*. The laundry would then be rinsed and put in a huge pot of starch. They were hung outside in a plot of land to air dry on nylon ropes. These ropes were entwined so tightly that each garment was suspended in between the ropes, eliminating the need for clothespins. When the wind blew, a psychedelic view of different colored saris, white and blue shirts, and pants of all kind, could be seen from afar.

It had been a while since Dukhiya's wife, Parvati, showed up to the house. She had not shown up during pick up or deliver of Raka's laundry.

"What happened to Parvati, is she all right?" Raka asked Dukhiya.

"She has been sick for quite some time, loves to stay in bed," he remarked in a matter of fact tone reflecting his lack of concern.

Raka could not help herself being concerned for the poor *dhobani*. She asked him again with a concern in her voice, "Did you take her to a doctor, to find out what was wrong with her?"

"No, it will cost me a lot to take her to the doctor. A little rest is all she needs," he retorted.

The next morning, Parvati showed up at the Raka's door holding her daughter's hand. There was no bundle of clothes with her this time.

Pleased to see her at the door, Raka inquired, "This has to be your oldest one, right?"

"Yes, Memsaab," she nodded and smiled enthusiastically. "After completing a few more years of schooling, she will start working for her father."

Raka could hear the daughter give a painful sigh, which was then immediately followed by a stern look by Parvati.

"Chup!" she scolded glaringly. "She used to enjoy going to school, but recently she has shown reluctance." Parvati was well aware that her daughter's classmates ridiculed her about being a child of a dhoba.

"Ma, do you know what they say at school? Why did she come to school, a *dhoba's* daughter, what will she do by studying? She should be washing and folding clothes."

"I want you to finish school and I want you to be able to read and write," Parvati said firmly, thinking about basic skills that she did not possess herself.

"Of course, she should finish her school before anything else," Raka agreed while placing a sweet relish into the little girl's hand.

Parvati took the weekly payment from Raka. She bowed her head and put her palms together, said 'Namaste,' and walked out gingerly. As Parvati left, Raka noticed that she was weak at her feet, her gait unusually slow as she leaned on her daughter's shoulder for support. The following week when she returned to collect money, Raka paid more attention and noticed then that the *dhobani* was pregnant with her fifth child and realized her body had taken a significant toll from her previous pregnancies.

The dhobani, along with her husband and four children, lived in a single room in a shanty house. Her husband, Dukhiya, had only two sources of happiness, sleep with his wife in their cramped room and have multiple children with hopes to add more working bodies to the family business. His insecurity was threatened whenever his wife rebuffed his advances or showed a lack of interest to meet his needs. For fear of reprisals, in the form of violent lashes and verbal outbursts, Parvati had no choice but to acquiesce to his desires eventually.

The eldest daughter, Lakshmi, practically raised her three siblings. She had been given the role of their second mother and often had to scold, spank, and even punish her younger two brothers and the youngest sister. She would be the one to clean up after each of them, and she also cooked and cleaned while her mother toiled in ironing.

One evening, Dukhiya came to Raka's apartment to collect laundry after a brief period of absence. Raka handed him the clothes one at a time giving him instructions. She noticed that the dhobi was unusually quiet.

"How's Parvati, did you take her to the doctor at all?" Raka asked him.

Dukhiya, with his eyes fixed on the floor, replied in a quivering voice, "We lost our baby. It was a boy, but he came too early. It all happened so quickly." He began crying, "I rushed her to the hospital, but it was too late. The baby did not cry after it was delivered, it was already dead." Large drops of tears fell on the ground near his bare feet. He quickly wiped off the tears off the ground with his toes, took the bundle from Raka's outstretched hands and walked off without looking up.

After a few months, there was another death in the *dhobi* family. It was Parvati who did not recuperate well from the complications of her childbirth. In addition to being chronically anemic and malnourished, her healthy quickly declined after she developed an infection from her delivery. It was difficult for Dukhiya to come to terms with his wife's untimely death. Perhaps it was remorse for not taking good care of his wife. The death seemed to be the catalyst in changing his life which had a profound impact on him. Although the enormous burden of the family now fell on Lakshmi, Dukhiya did his part to help her in every possible way, dividing his time between washing and doing chores. The dhobi became a responsible, heedful father in no time.

Meanwhile, Lakshmi decided to drop out of school. She could no longer cope with the enormity of her tasks at home and school work at the same time. One evening, however, she made her appearance to pick up Raka's laundry in company with another slender woman. Raka was pleased to see the little girl again, and more so puzzled to see the young woman with her.

With tears in her eyes, she introduced herself to Raka, "I am Parvati's cousin sister, she told me a lot about you and your kindness towards her family. I was called upon by Dukhiya to take care of his family when Parvati passed away."

Raka was equally curious to know about her. She was the unmarried cousin sister from the same village where Parvati grew up. After her brief stay with the family, for the convenience of his children, remarriage on Dukhiya's part seemed like an inevitable thing to take place. Within a short span of time, Dukhiya married Pootli, as he was so used to having help from his wife. He could not handle it once he became alone, especially because he could not afford to hire help.

For more than a year, content, if not happiness, was all that Pootli could bargain for from her marriage. She exerted all her abilities to please her new husband. Passive subservience and humility constituted a part of her duties as a wife. But very soon, he turned into a violent man whenever he was thwarted in his wishes. It was hard to break his old habit of drinking, and with stress and boredom he was at it again. He began to rely on it to take away all his hopeless feelings about life in general. Parvati had previously pressured him to quit drinking, which he did, but failed to keep up with that promise now. One evening when he came home from *dhobi ghat*, Dhukhiya walked in finding Lakshmi scurrying about in the kitchen; the single-roomed house was a mess and the children had not been fed even at the late hour. He felt the absence of their stepmother. Pootli had run away, deserting her husband and the children for another man.

One morning, Dukhiya showed up at Raka's house to pick up unwashed clothes from the housing complex.

"Unfortunately, I have no clothes for you today," said Raka.

The dhobi sat down on the floor, looking in her direction for some sort of explanation. Raka ushered him into the house and showed her brand-new washer and dryer.

"You don't need me anymore then, the machine will do all the washing and drying for you. But how are we going to survive if we lose business with you?" he said mournfully.

Raka explained that she needed a more reliable source of washing, but that from time to time, she would call the dhobi if she needed him. Both knew, however, this would be their last encounter. He left the premises of the apartment and continued to walk down the street to the next apartment who hadn't yet purchased the new technology that would slowly render his business useless. He grabbed the bag of clothes and headed off to the *dhobi ghat*, once again continuing his daily ritual of being a washerman.

GHUNGROO

IT SO HAPPENED THAT Suhashini's maid, in her desperation to find a job for her daughter, Kanchan, put a great deal of thought into the idea of her working in the same household to be a companion to Suhashini's daughter, Kinkini. She waited for an opportune moment when she could ask Suhashini. It was going to serve a dual purpose, she told herself, to have her own daughter close by and help her with an added income for her ever-growing family. She prided herself on the fact that Kanchan, although only two years older than Kinkini, was much more mature and intelligent.

She approached Suhashini one day and said meekly, "I've given this a lot of thought. If you allow me, can I ask you for a favor? I have a daughter who is close to your daughter's age and she is very good with her chores and sweet-natured, too. I think she'll be good company to Kinkini. She'll be happy if you just give her meals and few rupees in her hands."

Kinkini, who overheard the conversation from the dining room, immediately expressed her disapproval, "The last thing I need is a babysitter; I can manage my own."

"But Kinkini, this could be a great idea as it will be nice to have someone to be with you all the time, a friend and a companion perhaps," her mother said. "You can take her to your dance classes along with you." She continued, "Why don't you bring your daughter one day, and we can talk about the matter with Kinkini's dad."

To her mother's delight, Kanchan was hired without any hesitation. However, Kinkini quickly felt threatened and did not welcome her with open arms. When Kanchan began working in the house, she waited on Kinkini with much devotion and care beyond what was required. It was not easy for her to be patient with Kinkini, for the fact that she was very much of her own age. But to please her seemed to be the first and foremost desire in her life. Kinkini's whimsical behavior and temper tantrums were brushed aside as if they were wisps of hair. Each day was a challenge for the maid's daughter, but her tolerance grew every time a new episode pushed her on her edge.

It was a warm, blissful evening when a blue sky with patches of fleecy white clouds suddenly appeared after an unexpected soft spring shower. As the evening rolled on, the sun began its slow, beautiful descent into the horizon splashing its golden hue across the sky. The air was scented with a mild odor of an earthy-musty whiff of wetness after the rainfall. These odorants rose from the concrete and asphalt streets, but they were mixed with the aroma of freshly blooming spring flowers elsewhere in the city, promising a new beginning of life.

A typical lively, noisy street life emerged as soon as the rain stopped, as if the cessation of the rain had brought everybody back from their stupor. Vendors called out to buy their wares, crowds of pedestrians, shoppers and others could be seen walking along sidewalks outside the shops or trying to cross the road. The noise of cars zooming past, and hooting taxis was deafening. In the evening, the crowds multiplied as everyone from pedestrians to hawkers and commuters, quickened their pace, eager to reach home before it was dark. Stray dogs came out of their hideouts and started roaming the streets looking for scraps of food before nightfall.

Several years now had passed, and the two young girls, still on the cusp of their adolescence, sauntered lazily and carefree from Mayur Dance Academy, a well-regarded Kathak school specializing in classical dance.

"I'm glad the rain stopped as soon as class was over. I didn't want to be stranded at school," Kinkini said.

"Watch out now, you're walking too close to the curb, the drivers are so crazy they swish by you so fast," Kanchan warned Kinkini, laying a protective arm on her shoulders.

"You still sound just like Mother, but how many times have I told you, I'm old enough to keep an eye on oncoming cars. I'm not going to be hit by a car in broad daylight," Kinkini retorted and walked ahead while Kanchan tried to keep her pace.

Above their head, droplets of rain dripped from the branches whenever a breeze shook the trees. Deftly, they avoided each and every crevice puddled with muddy water along the path of the concrete road.

As Kanchan and Kinkini entered the house, they overheard Kinkini's parents arguing. "Kinkini spends hours at that dance school, when it's obvious that she is not motivated and that dancing isn't her passion," her father said. "Wouldn't it be more fruitful if we sent our daughter to math tutorial class rather than to a dance class? After all, what is she going to do with a degree from a dance school?"

Suhashini defended the idea of her daughter going for dance lessons, "When I was a little girl, I dreamt of taking dance lessons. But my parents were so conservative, they did not let me think about becoming a dancer. They told me that girls from the upper middle class did not dance in public. And I'm surprised that you sound just like my father." She continued to retort, "You are forgetting that Kinkini is only fourteen years old. She has an inborn talent, and I've seen her in the group dance they performed at their annual school function. I watched her intently, and I think she did far better than Shanti's daughter who doesn't even know how to dance."

Kinkini's father started to speak, but her mother cut him off.

"And they are spending additional private lessons hiring a teacher at home. With intensive training and practice, I am sure our daughter one day will be the greatest kathak dancer the world has ever known."

"We can hardly afford to keep a private tutor to give her dance lessons, whatever she is learning in school should be good enough," he said.

Suhashini had high hopes that her daughter would be a great dancer, but in reality, because her own dreams had been set aside, she continued to push her daughter. Her arguments eventually worked, and soon, her husband relented to her wishes of bringing home a private teacher. After all, she was a woman of strong determination and ambition.

The next day she took Kinkini and Kanchan to a shop to purchase a new set of *ghungroos*, rows of ankle bells worn during traditional dancing. They seemed to be of little interest to Kinkini as she gave a casual glance at them. Kanchan, on the other hand, picked up the shiny brass ankle bells, touching them gently and gave small shake, pleased at the rhythmic sound they made. The *ghungroo*, which formed an essential part of Kathak dance, were strung on a sturdy, thick cotton cord with each bell held in place by a special looped knot. They helped keep the dancer in tune to the music and stay in rhythm with the repetitive metrical, intricate footsteps. Suhashini bought the new set for her daughter knowing her first private dance lessons were scheduled for the following week.

The squabbles between Kinkini's parents did not abate. Rather, it often mounted to loud verbal altercations. One evening, when it was time to go to her class, Kinkini beckoned Kanchan to her side.

"Oh, Kanchan," she implored. "It looks like I misplaced

my new ghungroos, they are nowhere to be found," she said in an uncaring tone.

"I'll help you look. They may be under the bed," Kanchan said. "While sweeping the floor, I found one loose bell the other day."

Kanchan knew full well the fate of the ankle bells because Kinkini often pulled childish pranks to avoid going to her dance classes. She lifted the bedspread to look underneath Kinkini's bed.

"Here they are, but what have you done to them? They are loose and scattered all over," she said with a horrified expression. Kanchan picked up the loose bells and that afternoon walked all the way to the ghungroo shop, pleaded with the owner to fix them before Kinkini's parents came to know about the mischievous act. She watched carefully how the shop owner put all the bells back on the knotted cord, in case a situation like this occurred again, she could fix the bells herself.

The dance practices instructed by the private teacher were rigorous for Kinkini, but Kanchan loved them. She tried to finish her chores as fast as she could to be able to watch Kinkini practice. During those hours, she was transported into a world of ecstasy and joy. The tinkling chimes of the ghungroos and the rhythm of the dance steps transformed the world around her. She began to envisage herself on the same floor next to Kinkini joining in the practice. She was like a dancing doll, all keyed up, waiting to begin her graceful movements.

At the dance school, Kanchan chose a corner of the room, not too far from the teacher so that she could watch and listen to the lessons—and sometimes to perform the hand movements herself behind her back away from plain sight. Her receptive mind took note of all the details, and they remained embedded in her memory. The lessons brought a new sensation to her limbs, a quickening of her heartbeats, a desire and a new hope, and she was always transported only to be suddenly awakened from her reverie when the lessons were over.

One day Kinkini decided to go watch a movie with her friend Jhumur and skipped dance practice at the school. Kanchan repeatedly asked Kinkini to reconsider.

"Why don't you just go on behalf of me and tell me what I missed!" she said in a hurry as she ran off with her friend in the opposite direction of where they were heading.

Kanchan angrily walked to the dance school alone and sat in the corner as usual. In the middle of practice, something came over her and she let herself be carried away into this unknown world. With her eyes closed she made the precise facial expressions, perfected the movements down to her fingertips, and let the music completely take over her rhythmic movements. She danced away as if the entire room were hers, the floor moving beneath her feet with each delicate sound of the ghungroo bells bouncing off with a reverberating chime. She came out of her reverie suddenly, realizing she was in the middle of the dance floor in front of all of the students and the teacher herself. No one in the room moved and not a single ghungroo bell could be heard. A rush of heat hit Kanchan's face as she turned red glancing at herself at the practice room mirror. She immediately ran out of the dance school without looking back the entire way home, tears in her eyes of exuberance and fear of what she had just done.

The next day, Kinkini had heard from one of her schoolmates of Kanchan's rebellious dance performance. She confronted Kanchan after school.

"Where did you learn to dance? Everyone at school was talking about you today," she said angrily.

Kanchan kept her head down and didn't reply. Kinkini grabbed her ear and pulled her down to her level.

"Did you not hear me? Where did you learn to dance?!" she bellowed into her ear.

Kanchan pushed her away and blurted, "I learned with you ever since you first took lessons! I've been watching you during school, at home during private lessons, listening carefully to what the dance teachers have to say!" Her eyes began to swell. "I love dancing so much, but it gives me such sorrow to see that you don't even care about it."

Kinkini, still shocked that Kanchan had pushed her, yelled back, "I don't want you to ever come to dance school again. Otherwise, I will tell mother and send you back to your village so you can never work in our family again!"

Kanchan wiped away the tears on her face and nodded quietly. They both walked back home without saying any further word to each other.

As days slipped into months, Kinkini's dance practices began to slack more and more. One day, the dance teacher called upon her parents.

"I need to talk to you both Kinkini and her progress in her lessons. What I realized is that she is lagging behind other students. I'm afraid she isn't practicing enough," she said solemnly.

"But I see her practicing every day," Kinkini's mother contradicted her.

"She has to concentrate on her hand gestures and her eye movements. They are not coordinated. I will evaluate her competence in the forthcoming annual performance, but if you want her to continue, she must practice at least two hours a day. I believe Kanchan can help her with the eye and hand movements."

Her last sentence was a bombshell for both the parents. The very idea of Kanchan helping their daughter was preposterous.

"Kanchan! She is our maid's daughter, Kinkini's helper. What will she know about kathak dance?"

"It may be hard for you to believe, but Kanchan is actually a very good dancer. I saw her myself one day in school. I think if you let Kanchan guide Kinkini to practice at home together, she may improve," the teacher answered.

That night, Suhashini called Kanchan into the living room where Kinkini's would have her private lessons at home. She stood there with an old pair of ghungroos in her hand.

"Put these on. I won't ask again," she said quietly. "I want to see you dance."

Kanchan slowly picked up the ghungroo bells and placed them on each of her ankles. She moved to the middle of the room and closed her eyes. Slowly, she raised her arms and once again she imagined herself in a dark room with no one else. Her fingertips fanned out and she effortlessly danced with each beat of the ghunghroo bells. Suhashini was amazed that the maid's daughter had mastered the whole technique of the dance without a single lesson. She watched her dance with such emotion and crisp defined movements, in the same manner that she dreamed of doing herself growing up as a child.

"That is enough," Suhashini abruptly stopped Kanchan.

Kanchan stopped and stood there with her head down. "You will help Kinkini get ready for her performance at the end of the year. I want you to help coach her at home. You will not be allowed to go to dance academy school, nor will you practice by yourself. Do you understand?"

Kanchan quietly nodded without saying a word.

Over the course of several weeks, Kanchan slowly began helping Kinkini at home. At first, Kinkini was still angry at Kanchan for not telling her about her dancing skills. After a few weeks, she began to appreciate how good of a dancer Kanchan had become. They spent time after school and on the weekends dancing together synchronizing the sounds of the ghungroo bells. The two girls began forming a strong bond together, and more importantly, Kinkini finally began to love and admire the skillful art of Kathak dancing herself.

As the day of the graduating performance began to near, Kinkini had drastically improved. Her dexterity and positions were clean as she displayed a milieu of beautiful facial expressions, blossoming into a wonderful dancer. Even her dance teacher had noticed a significant improvement.

"What will I do without you, Kanchan? I honestly couldn't have done this without you. You are like my sister, I love you so much. What will happen next year when I have to leave for preparatory school?"

"Of course, I will always be there for you. Don't worry your little head, I will never leave you, not now nor ever," Kanchan assured her with a warm hug.

In no time, the day of the final graduating performance arrived. Kinkini was dressed in her dazzling outfit, ready for her debut. As Kanchan helped put the final touches on the beautiful outfit, Kinkini turned to her mother. "Can Kanchan come to the performance, too?"

"No, we'll be late, and she'll need to be here to warm up our food when we come home," her mother replied.

Kanchan gave an 'everything will be alright' look to Kinkini without uttering a single word and helped her quickly place the last set of bangles on her arms before the family hopped into a taxi and went off to the performance hall.

The night was unusually cold and windy with an overcast that covered the sky. Kanchan was a bright child and not unmindful of the risk she took when she left the house that evening and sped into the darkness of the road that appeared unfamiliar at night. She wiped her forehead with the back of her hand and climbed up the steps of the back entrance to the performance hall peeping in through the glass door. She watched Kinkini perform her solo dance flawlessly and clapped excitedly throughout each of her acts. When her final performance was nearly done, she hurried back down the stairs making sure she would have time to return back home before everyone else. As she quickly ran across the street in front of the performance hall, the bright headlights of an approaching car confused her, and she stood frozen in the middle of the road.

In the next moment, another magnificent light, much brighter than before, engulfed her. Her silent soul wrapped in the rainbow of sorrow, began to dance to the rhythm of the heavenly music surrounding her. She turned to look at the Earth, covered with darkness as she made her way around a great source of light, floating upward until she passed the stars far beneath her.

The Hindu belief says that there is a continuity of life after death, a single soul is reincarnated until it reaches a spiritual goal before returning to the supreme cosmic entity. When one returns back to this world, they start a new life in a different physical body to conclude the tasks that were important and left unfinished. Perhaps, it is at a different time point, a new unknown place, a new abode, surrounded by unfamiliar people one has never met before, other times, one finds a way back to a familiar home. It has also been described that there are times, one brings along similar traits of your character from your previous life. If the tasks remained undone, one is destined to come back again and again until freed from mortal obligations.

Kinkini found it hard to accept the sudden death of her friend Kanchan, and a gaping emptiness filled her young life. She missed her friend's presence in the house and at school. Having her at her beck and call, she called out her name every now and then. And every so often, she would awaken at night and let out a heart-wrenching scream.

On one of such nights, her parents rushed to her room and found her on the floor crying.

"Kanchan was here! I heard the jingling sound of ghungroos near my bed and now look at mine. See? They are neatly laid side by side on the night table. But I know I put them under the bed," she sobbed.

"No, Kinkini my little one, you are heartbroken without Kanchan," her mother assured her. "You must have been dreaming. You can sleep in our bed."

The family thought of hiring a new girl, but by then, Kinkini was self-reliant in all her activities and routinely continued to practice her dancing. With time, she overcame the loss of her friend. She grew into a responsible, mature girl far ahead of her own age. As years passed, she grew into a beautiful young woman, completing all her traditional dance training, and earned a degree that propelled her into a professional dancing career.

Twenty-two years later, Kinkini now a famous kathak dancer, was teaching in her own dancing school in a different city. She had travelled to different countries with her dance troupe and was the recipient of many international awards. In all her lecture demonstrations, she always recollected her days with Kanchan as a source of her inspiration and pivotal point in her childhood which changed her trajectory in life.

It was also said that Kinkini loved to talk about her daughter, Mira. She was always at her side, accompanying her mother at every show. It had been claimed that her daughter was also a child prodigy, completing the Kathak school of dancing as the youngest performer. Incredibly gifted, she never hesitated to find fault with the rhythm of her mother's steps, hand gestures, and the intricate movements of her body. With her small hands, Mira was beside every performance her mother performed, wrapping and unwrapping her mother's ghungroo. And even surprisingly, she knew how to fix them without anyone ever teaching her.

At times, Kinkini wondered how her daughter was so amazingly talented with such love and devotion toward Kathak dance, along with her genuine caring and affectionate personality. She glanced at her daughter who would always smile back in return, and thought perhaps Kanchan never left her, not even in death.

THE STREET PRINCESS

"LYNCH HIM! Hit him hard and teach him a lesson! Kick his crippled leg," one of the onlookers shouted.

I was curious, so I made my way through an excited, noisy, crowd and found a man lay on the ground. He was bleeding from a broken nose and a bruised face. Tears streamed from the eye that was not swollen shut, and blood ran down in rivulets down his contorted features. The eye that he could not open was purplish, bruised beyond recognition.

He murmured indistinct apologies from his badly cut lips, while his hands were up in the air trying to fight back by throwing few defensive jabs in the air. Bystander intervention to settle a dispute was common in the streets of Kolkata—or any other big city in India—and often the mob took control of the situation before the arrival of law enforcement.

At first, I thought it was a regular street fight. I craned my neck to see the extent of his injuries and started to intervene. Getting closer, it did not take long for me to recognize the unfortunate man. He was none other than the homeless rickshaw–puller who lived under the balcony of my apartment building with his wife and daughter, Rajkumari.

As I got close, I could smell the alcohol on his breath. He was totally inebriated, and I knew he beat his wife as a matter of course when under the influence of his regular hangovers. The beatings were often only stopped because of the intervention of local bystanders.

"Rajkumari, could you come upstairs for a little bit?" I beckoned her occasionally. She would come up always with a friendly smile and an expectation written all over her face as if she knew why I called her. She stood near the door and held out her shriveled, bony hands to collect the worn-out clothes I passed on to her.

Over the years, we became friends, and I had no way of knowing why I picked her out amongst all the nameless people that lived on the streets. Her name, which meant *princess* intrigued me – *a street princess?*

Rajkumari was born in the streets, grew up in the streets, and lived her life of misery underneath the balcony that provided the cover over her head. It was not even a shanty or a make-shift house or a shelter. Constant exposure to the ravages of weather had left indelible marks on the fine contours of her young face, which I believed would have been quite remarkable under different circumstances.

On a rainy day, one would find her standing upright under the balcony. Her sari was partially wet from ankle to her knees, with the rain splattering and spraying dampness, causing havoc around her. The only dry spot was the little space where she was standing. Her meager belongings were covered with a plastic tablecloth, topped with two or three red bricks to prevent it from being whipped away by the roaring wind. After the rain subsided, she would emerge from her hiding place, rinse out the wet portion of her sari, and light up the small *chula*, her earthen stove, and begin preparations for the evening meal of decayed vegetables, lentils, rice thrown into a pot.

My heart would go out to her on those rainy days when I came home from my classes, to find my mother waiting for me with a hot cup of tea and a dry towel in her hand.

Mother would fuss over me saying, "Why on earth did you forget your umbrella?" or "You should have taken a cab."

On such rainy days, Rajkumari's face often flashed before my eyes and without any hesitation I asked my mother, "Don't you think it will be nice to call Rajkumari up and offer her some tea?"

My mother, kind and generous as always, was receptive to the idea. She would add some chapatis to go with the tea. She was a crusader battling for the underprivileged classes, and I knew she would like to keep Rajkumari as a maid, but it was impossible. Rajkumari and her parents were Dalits, outcasts who belonged to the lowest class of society and to employ them in the household was preposterous and unthinkable.

Rajkumari had no caste, class or so to say, religion. She was even barred from stepping on the consecrated steps of a temple for fear of desecration and contamination. So, she was forbidden to worship in temples or draw water from the same well as caste Hindus. The feeling of distance was always starkly visible she avoided contact in everyday life.

So, it was with a mutual consent we kept our friendship within the boundaries of our social status. Some days, when the whole household retired for their afternoon siestas, my mother had Rajkumari come upstairs to sweep and dust. And mother always paid her generously. A chipped and nondescript plate was always kept aside for her. Whenever Rajkumari was offered food or drink, she would eat from the same chipped plate, and drink from the same broken handled cup. The maid's job was to handle the plate and cup, rinse them off, and set them aside for next time.

Rajkumari, along with her mother, took care of their alcoholic, crippled father. I had no idea what the woman's real name was, and Rajkumari never used her parents' given name, but I called her Dora because the torn and tattered sari that she wore had horizontal stripes and *dora* meant stripe in Bengali. Her husband had a broad toothbrush moustache completely shaved at the edges, so I called him Muchuwala. They were my neighbors, living so close yet so distant.

When he was young and still living in his village, Muchuwala had taken up his father's job of a rickshaw-puller. When the older man could no longer provide for his family, he was glad to relinquish the responsibility of his family on the shoulders of his eldest son. But unlike his father, Muchuwala moved to the big city where he could make more money.

Soon he was able to send money from his earnings back to his family on a monthly basis—until a road accident, a head on collision with a truck, crippled him for the rest of his life. He went back to his hometown for a recovery and to be with his family. It was during the time he was convalescing that he came up with an idea.

"We should move back to the city," he said to his wife. "We can try to carve out a living there, you may find a job and be able to earn some money. There are lots of opportunities in a big city!"

Dora had no reason to argue about moving to the city, and the prospect of earning money lighted up her spirits when there was hardly any source of income in the village. Once they arrived, she looked for menial jobs, aware that with her social position she could not hope for anything better. Big cities were less discriminatory than small villages, and soon she was hired to wash dishes in a busy, wayside eatery. Often, she was able to save leftovers to take home so the family would not go hungry.

In her spare time, she sorted plastic bags, bottles, containers from mounds of trash, and sold them in the markets of recycled commodities to make some extra cash for the family. At night, Dora made love to her handicapped husband under the vast expanse of the sky, groping for each other in the darkness of the night with nothing but a worn blanket to conceal them. And they brought Rajkumari into the world just the way my parents welcomed me into their world.

Soon after the birth of their child, however, the rickshaw-puller began to take refuge in alcohol, and soon he was addicted to a cheap alcoholic drink procured from fermented rice. He would come out of nowhere limping, staggering, and swearing with bloodshot eyes and would fling things aside that lay in his path, including his wife. In the morning light, Dora would cover herself with the end of her sari and try to conceal the bruises and marks left after the previous night's onslaught.

Drinking and punching his wife on a regular basis drew attention. Some people intervened and while in the process of rescuing her, the crowd pounced on him to set them apart. Later, Dora would feel pity towards her husband and tell the crowd to disperse and leave them alone, reminding them that it was a domestic affair. All I could see was a classic example of *Stockholm syndrome,* with the victim having soft feelings towards the perpetrator.

I thought to myself, maybe one day when I have a house of my own, Rajkumari could help me with my chores. I would teach her how to read and write, so that she could be independent and carve out a different life for herself. It was a vague thought, as elusive as the smell of a primrose.

Once I graduated, my parents, as was the norm, found a suitable husband and married me off. Whereas, Rajkumari, as she grew older, was hired to help in the kitchen by a nearby hotel owner who was always short of hands. Our lives took two entirely different paths over which I had no control, but providence had different plans.

On one of my visits to my parent's house, I learned that Rajkumari's parents were no more. The little space that they occupied under the balcony was devoid of any sign of habitation, it laid bare ready to be taken over by another destitute.

"What ever happened to Rajkumari?" I asked my mother. "She must be working in the same hotel, where do you think she could go?"

Since my mother had no idea, I had a talk with the hotel owner.

"She eloped, with one of my customers!"

The hotel owner didn't know any more, and I returned home with a heavy heart even though I was relieved to know that she found someone with whom she could begin a new life.

Years passed, and when my second child was on the way, I decided to stay with my parents for a brief period of time to be pampered and taken care of.

"Guess who was here?" My mother suddenly asked me. "Rajkumari!" My mother answered before I even had the chance to guess. "She left a note for you, probably had someone write it for her, but it's not safe for you to go and visit her in your present condition," my mother protested as if she could read my mind.

Using Rajkumari's hurriedly scribbled note and address, I made my way through a narrow alley of shanty dwellings made of scrap materials and corrugated metal, with open drains bordering both sides. Finally, I located her.

I was devastated to see her torn sari and emaciated face. She was destitute and starving because her lover had abandoned her for another woman. It was hard to believe she was driven into a life of abject poverty when she'd been willing to work so hard.

"You are going to come with me to help out with chores and help me take care of my little one," I said, without even thinking about the ramifications.

She nodded and a light glow came over her face like a sudden burst of sunshine on a cloudy day.

Her initial reaction when she entered my house was total bewilderment. She stood just inside the front door, toes rubbing against each other, not knowing how to act in the situation.

I gave her the servant quarters where I thought at least she will be safe, and over the next few weeks, I began to like her more and more, and in no time, she proved herself to be dependable, trustworthy, and not for an instant did I regret my decision to bring her into my house.

One day she surprised me by saying, "Will you please teach me how to read and write Didi?" Referring to me as her older sister was more of deference rather than our age, as she could be slightly older to me.

"Of course!" I answered.

So, our afternoons were full of zeal and enthusiasm of learning. With a copy of *Barnamala, Bengali book of Alphabets*, Rajkumari would repeat consonants and vowels after me, equivalents to English Alphabets ABCD. She surprised me with her learning abilities and in eight months duration she began to write small sentences.

In the meantime, my mother-in-law passed away and my husband's father began to live with his sons, shuffling six months with the older son, another six months with his younger son. It was our turn to have him stay with us for six months. He walked into the house and gazed at Rajkumari appreciatively.

"Where did you find this Goddess Durga?" he asked.

I made no reply to his comments. Instead I said, "Please wash up, you must be tired after your long journey."

But as days passed on, I began to notice his unbecoming attention towards Rajkumari. His eyes followed her everywhere and his glares embarrassed the poor girl. Some days, he would linger in the kitchen feigning to fetch a glass of water, always looking for an opportunity to talk to her.

At this moment in Rajkumari's life, when everything seemed to fall into place, a dark cloud appeared on the horizon of her content life. The cloud was in the shape of an old man with evil intentions. Her fresh budding youth and beauty brought about a resurgence of his carnal desires. His deep penetrating eyes seduced her several times in his perverse mind, creating a situation of uneasiness. She grew frightened.

I'm Dalit, an untouchable," she thought to herself. "Why would he want to have anything to do with me since he is from a higher caste? I want to talk about it to Didi, but it will only shock her."

One quiet afternoon, as she was washing and arranging the utensils on the rack, with her back to the dining area, she felt the brush of fingers on her back. She turned around to see the old man trying to pull her into a quick embrace, his lips caressing her cheek. She wrenched herself out of his grasp, stumbling and falling as she ran towards her room. A sudden sense of fear ran through her like the chill of an icy wind. In another incident, she woke up the entire household when she let out a frightful shriek in the middle of the night. When confronted, she conjured up a story and insisted she had been dreaming. But she knew she had seen the shadow of the old man near her bed.

Soon, my father-in-law turned into a vicious, frustrated old man, and in order to avenge himself, he was increasingly cruel to Rajkumari. He told me to get rid of her, that a girl belonging to a low class should not be working in a respectable family.

"Tell her to get her stuff and look for another job, some place suitable for her." He said angrily.

"No," I answered back. "She is a very reliable person and it is hard to get someone who is so trustworthy and efficient."

Eventually, his persistence for not having her in the house pushed him to concoct wrongful accusations against Rajkumari.

One morning he came up with a story which stirred up a big commotion in the house.

"I lost my gold ring," he said, "It was on my night stand table. I remember distinctly where I put it. It just can't disappear into thin air."

Everyone started to look all around the houes in the hope of finding the missing ring. The old man after a while entered Rajkumari's room and took the ring out from underneath her pillow to accuse Rajkumari of stealing the ring.

She lowered her face not daring to look at anyone and said. "I did not take the ring, and I did not put it under my pillow". With tears in her eyes she fell upon my feet, "Didi, believe me I did not take the ring; I did not go to his room to sweep or dust."

Before I could say anything on her behalf my father-in-law began pulling out her belongings from her room. "Leave this house at this moment, or I will have you arrested for stealing!"

I squeezed Rajkumari's shoulder and gathered up my courage to confront the vindictive old man.

"Father, it is time for you to go back to your other son's house and live there. Rajkumari will stay here, for this is her house, too."

With that I started picking up her belongings and put them back in her room while he looked on in astonishment.

REPRESSED MEMORIES

"HI MOM," SAMEER SAID as he walked through his parent's front door, encircling his mother in a warm hug. Since he lived in Delhi with his wife and children, he didn't visit his parents in Patna very often, so his mother greeted him with much enthusiasm. His father, on the other hand, gave him a perfunctory look devoid of emotion. He was preoccupied with lifting up the couch cushions, apparently looking for something.

"What are you looking for?" Sameer asked.

"My reading glasses. They probably slipped under the cushions. Never mind I'll find them later."

The next morning, Sameer's father went rummaging through the papers and magazines on the coffee table because he thought he lost his key ring.

"Here I'll help you look," said Sameer as he joined his

dad looking at probable places where the key ring could have been misplaced. Soon he noticed the contours of the key ring inside his father's coat pocket.

"It's been there the entire time, Dad," Sameer laughed it off. "You need to slow down."

Sometime later that day, he saw his father standing beside his bed mumbling to himself. "I know I put my reading glasses on the nightstand, but they're not there anymore."

"They are on top of your head, Dad," Sameer joked.

Sameer's father held an important position at a financial institution and had begun having memory lapses, forgetting people's names at work, and finding it difficult to do the simplest tasks that he had been doing for years. And now, he constantly asked where his things were. One time he was late for work looking for his favorite pen which was neatly tucked into his shirt pocket. Another time, he told his wife to fire the help because he thought they'd stolen his watch even though he hadn't taken it off it since he bought it ten years earlier. Some days, he complained that he could not remember the right words in the right context, or he could not remember what he was going to say. He was frustrated when he couldn't remember the names of people he just met. He had not been worried until recently, when he began failing to understand finances, accounting technologies, and even basic math. He gradually realized he could no longer deal with the family paperwork. Payments were delinquent unintentionally or sometimes bills were not paid at all.

Sameer and his mother made light of his symptoms of memory failure and joked that age had finally caught up with him.

"Don't worry, Dad," Sameer reassured him. "It's just part of getting old."

His father couldn't let his worry go, so Sameer helped make an appointment with the family doctor. He was evaluated for memory impairment, and a follow up test six months later confirmed a diagnosis of mixed dementia with Alzheimer's disease. It was an unexpected blow for everyone and sounded like an unnatural echo to Sameer's ear. But there was nothing one could do, aside from not give up hope, as doctors were working hard to come up with new treatments to arrest the progress of the disease.

Six months later, Sameer visited again and realized things had deteriorated rapidly. It was an uphill battle for his mother when she decided to be her husband's sole caregiver. She quit her job as a teacher, and now was stressed out, depressed, and overwhelmed knowing that it would continue to get worse in the years to come. At one point, Sameer's father took him into the bathroom, locked the door, and whispered, Sameer, your mother tried to kill me. She put poison in my food, I don't trust her. She even choked me while changing my clothes. I need someone else, not her."

Sameer tried to sooth him, "No Dad, Ma would never do that. She loves you."

Soon, his father became verbally abusive and aggressive when he felt helpless or afraid. Often when he was being bathed or dressed, he would kick, hit, or bite his wife. As his disease progressed, his mood swings got worse. At one moment he was calm and gentle, perfectly fine, and the next moment he was howling for no apparent reason. He snapped at her several times when she disagreed with him over minor things. At times he would act more like a child when he went to the grocery store with her, buying things at the store when he already had those at home.

One day his mother discovered a long trail of red ants from the cupboard underneath the kitchen sink. On investigation, she found a mound of candy wrappers, jam packets, and stockpiled sugar packets.

"Sameer, look what I found under the sink. Your dad is saving these sugar packets and ants are invading the house. He could have asked me if he had a craving for sweets!"

"No, Ma," Sameer said. "This is common in old age. Dad feels insecure sometimes and doesn't want to bother you."

Sameer finally sought assistance through an agency and tried to hire someone to help his mother cope with being a full-time caregiver. But she would not let a stranger come to her house and did not accept any help from anyone else as she did not trust anyone but her son. It was hard on her, and on his visits, Sameer often found his mother angry and in tears. He thought she might be slipping away, too.

Finally, two and a half years from the date of his father's diagnosis, Sameer moved his family to Patna so he could be with his father at his final stages of his disease and look after his mother as her health had been declining as well.

"Dad, don't you think it was a good decision for us to move back to Patna?" he asked one afternoon as he propped his father up in bed. "I am much closer, and I can help take care of you and Ma."

"I must have seen you somewhere. What did you say your name was?"

Sameer read to his father every night and watched helplessly as his father's health declined. He was fading fast, and death was just a matter of time. Sameer made him comfortable in every possible way, until he gradually went into coma and was gone within a few days.

Sameer had to focus on caring for his mother next. How to ease his mother's grief and make her life happier was the foremost thought in his mind. She moved in with Sameer's family and it was the presence of her son, daughter-in- law, and children that helped to a certain extent to ease her pain and bereavement. But underneath the calmness, there were signs of grave depression at the loss of her beloved husband. It manifested itself in different aspects of her life. She began to show decreased interest in all her favorite activities and got annoyed at the slightest disagreement.

One week, Sameer took his mother on a pilgrimage to Kashi, the holy site for devotees in Benares. The trip was a nice diversion for both of them, and she seemed happy away from the surroundings of her home. After her return from Kashi, however, she fell back into the same sad, reclusive mood. After being a caregiver for so long, she felt as if her life was directionless, as if it had no meaning or purpose.

Then all of a sudden, one evening Sameer noticed his mother all dressed up in one of her fine silks.

"Look at you, Ma. So beautiful! That silk brings color to your face."

She laughed happily and told him he certainly knew how to please his mother.

"I have been waiting for your dad to come home, so that we could both go to the store. I need a few things to replenish my pantry".

Not knowing how to react, Sameer stood still, completely flabbergasted at this sudden and drastic change of behavior on his mother's part. But he composed himself, took her hands gently in his own hands.

"Dad left us forever to be with God, Ma. I can take you wherever you want to go."

"No, you're lying to me. He's been gone only for a short while, and I will wait for him with or without you," she retorted.

He saw his mother's frail form shaking with gasps and sobs, stuttering with each word she was trying to say, conveying a sense of hopelessness. His own eyes welled with tears as he enveloped her in his arms.

A few years after his father's death, when everything seemed to fall back into place, there were subtle but noticeable changes in his mother's lifestyle. She left things lying around in the house because she could not remember where they went, and she started imagining things, mixing up facts, hiding her possessions. She was paranoid that something was going to get her. Her strange and suspicious behavior became a matter of concern when she kept closing the drapes of her bedroom even during the day. She often forgot to take a shower and wore the same clothes day after day. When Sameer prodded her to make sure she took care of herself, she got angry.

"I don't want to take a bath. I took one yesterday." She protested.

Sameer tried to soothe his mother to avoid a confrontation, but worried about her health, and her deteriorating mental condition. After a lot of coaxing, there was a breakthrough when she finally changed her mind about seeing a doctor. The occasional forgetfulness, a little repetition, defensiveness and denial showed Sameer that she had the same symptoms that had afflicted his father.

She was diagnosed with Lewy dementia. For Sameer, this was history repeating itself. At the time of his father's illness, his mother was the sole caregiver. Now, she was slowly being transformed into a totally different human being. He hired caregivers to be at the house when she started having trouble signing her name, had accidents, and even falls that landed her in the emergency room. She surprised her caregivers with lewd remarks, screamed when they tried to feed her, and often threw her food at them. Caring for her at home became exhausting. For her safety—and for his own family's sake—she needed long-term care in an assisted living facility. Sameer searched his mother's familiar, loving face, but she was not there anymore. Instead what he saw was a dangerous and deranged woman who sometimes didn't know him and who was often oblivious to her surroundings.

The residence he found was small with 30 patients, who needed full-time care. The patients were grouped together according to their physical and mental state. Although the facility was staffed with kind and skilled care providers, they remained confined, shut away, sometimes forgotten.

"How do you feel this morning? Did you sleep well?"

The head nurse spoke softly as she smoothed the pillows of each and every patient. The hourly nursing checks included lifting the residents from their reclining positions, changing their incontinence pads, removing their bedclothes, changing into fresh ones, giving them sponge baths, and dressing them. Then each patient was transferred into a wheelchair and pushed into the day room where others gathered around a central table for morning breakfast.

It was a huge transition for Sameer's mother. She was now surrounded by strangers in a new place, with no knowledge of the people who were changing her clothes and feeding her. To catch sight of her son—when she recognized him—was always a relief for her. His visits let her know that he still cared for and loved her and that she was not alone.

"Take me home, I do not like it here. If I stay here, who is going to cook for your dad? I want to eat things I like." She continued to say when Sameer came to visit her. Eventually she made herself comfortable at the facility.

After several uneventful days in the facility, a new development began to take shape. She was obsessed with things happened in her past and would get worked up over them. She could suddenly remember vivid details of occurrences that took place years before.

At the facility, certain mental exercises were added to patient activities. They were encouraged to solve puzzles, read, write, draw and paint—anything that would keep the mind working and challenged. Knowing she was an art teacher, the nurses encouraged her to draw pictures of anything that would make her happy. She surprised the staff one day by drawing the picture of an infant wrapped in a blanket. She drew the same picture over and over again.

"That's my baby girl," she said and smiled happily.

"Oh, she's gorgeous! She must have grown into a pretty woman. Where is she now? Is she coming to see you soon?" The nurse kept asking questions to keep the conversation flowing.

"She lives far away, but maybe Sameer can bring her. I have not seen her for a long time. She will not know me, but I love her a lot. They did not want her, they told me get rid of her, threw me out of the house because I had her." She rattled on, becoming overwrought with emotion and helplessness.

At night she was afflicted with her tremors.

"I had scary dreams, maybe I should go home," she told the nurse when she came to check on her. Her nightmares occurred almost every night. The doctor later explained to Sameer that she had come to a point when she may be hallucinating and might experience delirious and family misidentifications.

One evening she was sitting with her head bowed, in the living room of the facility when Sameer walked in with his daughter.

"That's my husband and my daughter," she told her nurse.

At the next drawing session, she drew a picture of an old house, with a walled garden and dense trees in the back of the house. She pointed at the house and claimed it was her house. When Sameer saw the drawing, he could not believe that his mother could reproduce such an exact replica of the house he grew up in, his grandparents' home. She was being haunted by her remarkable memory, an incredible phenomenon, he thought.

She drew the same picture over and over again, but to everybody's amazement, her *repressed memories* added a new feature to the masterpiece. A small, slightly elevated patch of land in the garden, covered neatly with flowers.

All the efforts of doctors and nurses could not stop the natural progression of the disease. It was not long before she began to lose control over her bodily functions. One morning, the nurse went to wake her up, but she did not respond. She was gone. Sameer was desolate, and for a long time, he could not talk without tears in his eyes.

Sameer's only aunt, his mother's younger sister ,came to do the last rites and to be with her nephew at the moment of bereavement. He was unprepared for his aunt's burst of tears when she threw her arms round his neck and declared, "I'll love you more from now onwards." He wrapped his arms around her and cried long and heartily.

After he and his aunt had taken care of all of his mother's dear possessions, he said, "How about if we all go and have a look at our old house?"

Sameer was very young when he lived in his grandparents' house, so he did not remember the details of the house. It was now an old, red brick dilapidated looking home with a sagging roof that was ready to give way in a strong wind. The cement on the front porch was crumbling and some of the windows had no glass in the wooden frames. But the structure of the house was strong, reminding Sameer of a beautiful place that had seen better days. As he stood in the kitchen, memories of his childhood summers rushed back to him. Out of curiosity, he went to have a look at the garden that was neglected over the years. The grass was allowed to grow long, concealing the mossy path that led into the interior of the garden. He was amazed beyond measure when he recognized the small patch of land that his mother portrayed in her drawings. It was slightly elevated, covered with overgrown, flowering plants.

"Do you know anything about this little mound in our garden?" he asked his aunt. She looked away at first, and then began to pour her heart out to her nephew.

"It had been a well-kept secret and an unfortunate occurrence during your early childhood years. It was hushed up and forgotten as an untold sad part of our lives. Over the years your parents did not want to divulge this information to you, because they were afraid that you might confront them with questions. The truth is that you had a sister who died in her infancy and the circumstances leading to her death were shrouded in mystery."

"A sister?" Sameer couldn't believe it, but his aunt didn't answer. She just went on with the story.

"The family expected a boy, so when your mother gave birth to a baby girl, your father's parents were displeased and took the baby from her. It was a terrible and cruel custom, but they feared that keeping a daughter would mean they would have to pay a large dowry when it came time to wed her. They would not acknowledge the birth of a girl in the house, especially when they lived in such poverty already." She paused for a moment but then continued, "The baby was taken away from your poor mother the moment she was born, and she never saw her again."

His aunt was totally exasperated and let out a sigh of relief.

"What? What do you mean?" Sameer exploded in anger. "How is it that Ma never mentioned I had a sister? How could she cut out such an important part of her life?"

How he wished his mother had told him everything. He instinctively ran to the back of the garden and grabbed a shovel. He went to the small mound and started digging. He did not have to dig too deep until he struck upon a soft object—the remnants of a baby quilt, made with small squares of faded pink and green fabric. He carefully picked up the quilt, gave it a gentle shake, and watched as tiny bones dropped at his feet. He confirmed his disbelief. Without saying a further word to his aunt, he quickly put back the remains back into the quilt and gently laid it back into the small grave, covered it back up, and went home.

THE BARREN WOMAN

THE VILLAGE CALLED Koramundi was one of the thousands of rural areas bordering Andhra Pradesh, and Orissa, in the southeastern part of India. Its inhabitants were mainly tillers of the soil. Some of them, the lucky ones, came into possession of acres of land thus proclaiming their status as rich farmers. There existed a village council, and besides settling disputes regarding possession of lands and properties, it also presided over the domestic affairs of the villagers. In other words, these highly controversial councils control all aspects of rural life. So, for decades, these families in the cluster of villages lived under the laws imposed by a group of unelected but powerful men, and there was controversy about the violent nature of the punishments they meted out to wrong doers.

At this moment, a group of village elders were discussing the fate of a farmer's unfortunate wife. The allegation brought against her was grievous—her inability to give her husband a child—and that, moreover, the wife and her lies had misled and tricked the farmer into marrying her. The allegation seemed to be strong one in this case since a farmer's wealth was reckoned not by the acres of land he possessed, but by the number of children he reared.

In the first few years of her married life, Sonal, the farmer's wife, was showered with special care with the expectations that she would bear children. Natural and herbal treatments were amply given to overcome her inability to conceive. She was given the tender roots of banyan tree, tender leaves of blackberry fruit, nuts, raisins and figs, but nothing worked. She was unable to give the farmer a child.

In ancient times, the Egyptians and Mesopotamians sought divine assistance and practiced fertility rituals to beget a child. These were commonly associated with pagan practices, fertility rites and ceremonies that were believed to improve chances of conceiving. The deities played a crucial role throughout the process of childbirth, from conception to delivery. Not only the barren women, but also the women who had already given birth would pray for fertility.

In the Hindu pantheon, Ma Shashti, represents the Goddess of Fertility and bestows children to those women who propitiate her with rigorous prayers and ritualistic oblations. In order to be blessed by her, Sonal took her bath every morning and performed her pooja with much fervor. She also helped feed the hungry children in the village once a week. But nothing seemed to work for her.

The theory that every malady that seized a woman was caused by an evil spirit or by an angry God flourished in rural India. The village councilmen, who were all superstitious and uneducated, believed in witchcraft and sorcery as the answer to all afflictions, so, they concluded that the farmer's wife needed to be treated by the holistic doctors locally known as Ojhas. The Ojhas claimed to possess supernatural powers enabling them to drive away evil spirits, and they knew various spells and modes of incantations. For instance, to cure barrenness, they had a spell meant to remove the obstacles to conceiving a child.

Also, it had been known from ancient days that flagellation was supposed to have the power of scaring demons, the Ojhas brought the farmer's wife under the old *pipal* tree to inflict lashes on her until the demon preventing her from becoming pregnant left her body. They started with gentle blows at first, then gradually increased the severity of the lashes so that the demon would be tamed and released from her body. There were cheering bystanders watching the whole scenario, even though some were skeptics who knew the Ojhas were making money out of gullible and vulnerable people.

Customarily, a woman in India is often addressed or introduced by her son's given name.

Even her husband, while showing love and respect, might refer to his wife as his son's mother.

And a son's mother always hoped for grandchildren.

"I hope I will be able to see my grandchild's face before I die," her mother-in-law said with sarcasm in her voice. Her daughter-in-law was not blessed with the famous statement – *may you be the mother of hundred sons.* It was a sad situation for Sonal.

After a few years, the farmer's younger brother married a girl from a neighborhood village, and within a short period of time, she blessed her husband with a son. This was not a joyful event for Sonal. In fact, it had an adverse effect on Sonal's not so favorable position in the family. The birth of a son heightened her sister-in-law's status in the family, a position to be envied and enjoyed with pride even as Sonal, was frowned upon and humiliated. A social stigma was attached to her condition of barrenness. As a result, she rarely went out of the house as she was shunned as an inauspicious person. Even if her shadow fell on a passerby or crossed the path, or had an encounter with her, first in the morning, the person had to make a penance by taking a bath in the river. Her presence and her touch came to be regarded as an ill omen, incurring the wraths of the almighty. In religious gatherings, weddings, baby showers and other happy occasions she was required to stay away and was not allowed to enter the room where a woman would be delivering her baby as she might cast an evil eye on the unborn child.

The village of Koramundi, although tucked in between two larger villages, had the conveniences of a modern life, like electricity and water, concrete roads, an elementary school, medical facilities, and buses. And it so happened that one day a team of young and enthusiastic doctors came to the village for their mandatory service in the rural areas. In due time, they set up their clinic and offered their free medical service to the villagers.

One late morning, Paresh, the youngest and most intelligent resident doctor in the group, was on his way to see an old sick man at his clinic. He was distracted by something that caught his attention immediately. A group of men and women were hovering over an unconscious woman, presumably in her early thirties, beaten up badly with a cane by a village doctor, the Ojha.

"Where is her husband?" The young doctor asked in bewilderment. He looked around for an answer. The crowd pointed at a rustic looking young man. Paresh took him aside and said, "Come to my clinic tomorrow, I want to see you and your wife in the morning. And tell them to stop beating your wife. You will end up in jail if she dies."

The next morning the farmer took his wife went to the clinic and had a long conversation with the young doctor. The doctor ran several fertility tests and told them to come back the next day. When they returned, Paresh took him aside and said, "We sent your wife's specimen to a fertility specialist and ran ultrasound tests when she was ovulating, and everything seems to be normal. Your tests, however, are not normal. You have a hormonal imbalance, you need to undergo treatment, we recommend that you go to the city and see a specialist. Your wife is not to be blamed for not being able to give you a child!"

The farmer shook his head, refusing to believe the doctor. "No, it can't be me. My father is healthy, my brother's wife just gave birth to a healthy son. It's not true. Tests can be messed up. I want Sonal to undergo more tests."

"The tests are accurate," the doctor insisted. "If you really care for your wife and want a child of your own, we can start the treatment immediately."

The next day, the farmer sent his wife to the clinic to run more tests, the doctors refused and told her to go home and send her husband back.

Kishan and his family refused to believe what the doctor had told them about his condition. Instead, the parents arranged for a second wife for their son. They went to great lengths to secure another bride so that a son and heir could be provided. Kishan's father had one of the largest landholdings and was anxious that inheritance of the land should stay within the family.

One early morning, her belongings were gathered up. She fell on her knees pleading, "Please don't send me away, I will be more rigorous with my fasting and will do anything you want me to do to bear a child for you."

But they already made up their minds of sending her away. Her own parents did not welcome her back. She was a burden to them, and so she was subjected to constant humiliation. "Sonal, you are a *barren woman* and the doors to heaven are closed for you," Her aunt remarked one day. "Who is going to light your funeral pyre?"

The matter came to a pinnacle moment when her youngest cousin sister was to be married, her own aunts and uncles did not want to have her around the joyous occasions, and she was asked again to leave the house. Sonal eventually left the house to go to the adjoining village where people were a little more progressive than in her own village.

In the meantime, the farmer brought home his second wife, a younger bride with the hope that she will bear children for him. But because of his adamant nature, he refused to undergo treatment and he remained childless. The second wife again was subjected to similar fertility rituals, ceremonies that were believed to improve chances of conceiving. Special elaborate offerings were made to gods and goddesses of fertility to ward off inauspiciousness and "hindrances" from the body. Several years passed, but nothing worked. The farmer remained childless.

It so happened that one morning the farmer went to the adjoining village to visit his childhood friend Arvind, whom he had not seen for many years. Arvind was happy to see him, after they caught up with the latest news, he asked the farmer to stay for dinner. During their conversation, a young boy of three or four appeared.

"Mother sent me to tell you that dinner is ready, you and your friend can join us to eat."

"Sure, my boy," Arvind answered.

Then he turned to the farmer and introduced his little boy. "This is Rajan, my son, who has just turned four."

As the farmer sat down to eat, he saw a familiar face bringing food for him on a platter. Although the face was partly covered with the end of her saree, it was not hard for him to recognize the face of his first wife, Sonal.

Seeing him, she dropped the platter and ran into the kitchen. Arvind, in utter disbelief ran after his wife and found her sitting curled up in a corner sobbing uncontrollably.

"That's my husband who threw me out of the house for not giving him a child. Send him away! I don't want him near my house."

"Calm down Sonal. How can I be rude to him he is my friend! I had no idea that my old friend was your husband. He seems to be a nice person. I think it was because of his family who pressured him to get rid of you," Arvind tried to console her.

"He didn't speak up for me! He didn't believe the doctor and refused to get treated for his own problems. Instead he blamed me for not being able to have a child," Sonal retorted in between her cries.

Arvind stepped out of the kitchen to rejoin his friend, but the farmer had already left. He ran after him and saw his friend waiting at the bus stop.

"Listen," Arvind said, "when I found Sonal she was in a very bad shape, completely emaciated, her clothes torn and tattered, she was living in the streets. I took her to my sister's house for food and shelter. My sister asked me what kind of monster could abandon his wife and leave her to die in the streets! She slowly recovered and in no time and at my sister's suggestion, I married her and brought her home. She is a kind person and a good wife, and I feel very lucky to have found her. And she is a good mother."

There were tears of remorse in the farmer's eyes, and he boarded the bus for home without a word.

The episode of his visit with his friend and accidental encounter with his first wife brought about a change in him. As he came to his senses, he stopped blaming his second wife for not having a child. He went to the clinic to undergo treatments.

Two years later, there were festivities in the rich farmer's house, the entire village came to celebrate the birth of Kishan's first born, a male child. Arvind, too, came with his wife Sonal and son Rajan. Soon, Paresh and his young team of doctors left the village. Their rural services were done.

THE GAMBLERS OF SHANTIPUR

RAMKANT WAS BORN into a family of gamblers in a village called Shantipur, in Uttar Pradesh, found in the northeastern part of India. His grandfather was a compulsive gambler who carelessly increased the stakes of his betting, forfeiting all his material and personal assets. He wanted to become rich overnight and lived with the hope that some chance win would change his entire life. That chance never happened.

There was a rumor amongst the villagers that Ramkant's grandfather had died of unnatural circumstances, shrouded in great mystery that remained unsolved. Ramkant's father, too, died an ignominious death due to gambling, leaving his young family in abject poverty.

Ramkant's mother, Gayatri, tried hard to dissuade her son from following the footsteps of his forefathers, whose notoriety spread into the neighboring villages. She hoped that he would one day stand on his feet and earn back the good name of the family. Otherwise, she feared finding a bride for him would be a problem.

With the help of relatives, Gayatri set up a kirana, a small local grocery store, on the roadside, and Ramkant went to school in the early hours of the morning, so that he could help his mother at the store in the evenings. Unfortunately, Ramkant proved to be a great disappointment. He was an underachiever who lived only on the support of others. He had to stay in each class for two to three years before being promoted to the next grade, and by the time he finished school, he was past twenty.

Once he began job hunting, Gayatri held her breath and waited by the door, eager to get a glimpse of a happy face when he returned home. But instead, she saw only slumped shoulders and downcast eyes. Sometimes his footsteps sounded heavy, reluctant to take another step or he behaved as though he was carrying the weight of the world on his shoulders. People hired him for small odd jobs, but he could not hold them for longer than a month.

Eventually he started working full time at his mother's grocery store. Ramkant kept himself busy buying and selling fresh vegetables from the market, stocking up shelves with other commodities that people needed every day. Seeing her son involved in the business made his mother happy.

By now, Ramkant was thirty-four and still not married. In the villages, people start gossiping if you were not married in the late twenties or thirty at the most, so Gayatri needed to find a bride for her son. But no one was willing to tie the knot with him, there were no good responses from any girl in the village. Because of the paucity of girls in the village, a marriage broker was called upon to assist in the search for a bride. Eventually, Ramkant went to a neighboring village and bought himself a bride for the sum of 4,000 rupees.

Over the years, Gayatri's success in the business raised the admiration of the neighbors and friends. And yet there appeared a dark cloud rising from a direction of which she was not aware of, a disruption in the normal pace of her life. Her astute mind discerned discrepancies in her accounts. Money that came from the store started to disappear, and she detected inconsistencies in the ledger book.

It started with small amounts but the discrepancy in earnings continued to grow. When confronted by his mother, Ramkant invariably tried to convince his mother that the money was used for store purposes. Buying and selling back vegetables at a higher price was becoming a profitable business for them. Some people came to the store just to buy them and they were gone before noon.

One morning Gayatri said, "Ramkant, I didn't have enough money to buy fresh vegetables today. What happened to all the extra money we made selling vegetables? I thought I would set aside a part of the profit to repair our leaking roof."

Ramkant promptly answered, "Don't worry, I was going to the market to buy some fresh vegetables."

In the meantime, Gayatri started to take the cash earned at the store home each night, stowing it underneath her mattress. But after few weeks, she found 500 rupees were missing from the hidden money.

Ramkant became defensive when he was accused. "That's my money, too! I worked hard, and I needed 500 rupees to buy things for my wife. If you don't believe me ask Tamanna. She is the one always nagging me for money!"

"So, now you are blaming me," Tamanna cried out. "I never ask money from you! You don't have anything. It's always your mother who's buying me all the necessary things." Both his mother and his wife were dumbstruck by his blatant lies.

Gradually household items began disappearing. One day, Gayatri's silver anklets were gone. Then, a pair of gold earrings that Tamanna kept in a lentil jar for fear of burglars went missing. Tamanna suspected Ramkant for stealing her earrings but did not mention it to her mother-in-law for fear of Ramkant beating her.

Another time, Gayatri stood in the kitchen shaking her head. "Where were the two brass pots that I bought at the fair? They are brand new. I didn't use them at all, and now I see they are gone!"

"What brass pots are you talking about?" Ramkant said. "There are no brass pots here. I don't know when you bought them. Maybe you pawned them. You don't remember anything nowadays. Besides, maybe Tamanna has given to her sister."

One late afternoon, Tamanna was washing and cleaning the utensils near the water tap at the back of the house when two rogues appeared from nowhere and grabbed her from behind. She let out a scream and tried to fight them back.

"Ramkant owes us money," one said in her ear. "Why don't you be nice to us? After all, he is the one who sent us to you. Otherwise, how would we know where you live?"

She managed to escape and ran frantically inside, hid herself in one of the inner rooms, and bolted her door. She wept silently as she realized that her husband was willing to sell her to strangers to pay his debts.

After that attack, Gayatri decided to finally take action. Ramkant left the house one Sunday afternoon, when the store remained closed. He told his wife that he had some errands to run, but as evening rolled around, he did not return. His mother stood outside, hoping to ask somebody if they had seen Ramkant. One of her neighbors pointed towards the store.

On reaching her grocery shop, Gayatri found her son bending over a pack of cards. He was with a group of men playing game of *Teen Patti*.

She let out a mournful cry at the terrible revelation. With bitterness in her voice, she told Ramkant, "I tried so hard to keep you away from this vice, but I failed and now I know the truth about the disappearance of all my hard-earned money". She gave a hard look at her son and realized with a broken heart that he had been stealing from her.

She went home and collected the rest of the money she'd stowed away beneath her mattress. She put the money in a cloth bag and hid it in the most secret place she could think of—the back of her house, in the dense undergrowth of a mango tree.

She checked the cloth bag every day to see if the money was stolen and began to notice that the drawstrings of her bag were loosened, and a small portion of her money gone.

Ramkant, like a cunning fox, found out her new hiding place. Still, she left the money in the same place because she couldn't think of where else to hide it.

It so happened that one day a snake charmer passed by her house, balancing his serpents in baskets hanging from a bamboo pole slung over his shoulder. The villagers came out and gathered round him for an entertainment. He sat down and started to play a pungi flute while he prodded a coiled snake in his basket.

Some children in the crowd even tried to open the basket in their eagerness. The music from the flute, with the light prodding from the charmer, the cobra slowly uncoiled itself from one of the baskets. It stood up with its hood all spread out and started swaying to the tune of the flute.

The cobras were natural guardians of treasures, when threatened, instead of retreating they would hold and defend their ground. Gayatri, like other village women believed that a snake could guard her hidden money underneath the tree. So, she went up to the snake charmer, offered him some money and whispered words into his ears. The snake charmer shook his head vigorously disagreeing. At first, he refused to comply with her suggestions but, finally, he relented. He smiled in approval and acquiesced to leave the baskets with the snakes at the back of her house, near the mango tree. Snake worship still prevailed in India, and superstitions and beliefs about snakes could still be found. Steeped in village folk ideas, Gayatri performed the rituals needed to appease the snake God. She did not forget to put her bundle of money under the thick mango grove, and in fact, she made it heavier as she put all her savings inside the pouch.

That night, the people of Shantipur had a peaceful night, not a leaf on the trees stirred, even the night creatures stopped howling as if with a tacit understanding. It was a full moon night, and the moon was an omen. Gayatri gazed at the rising moon with vacant eyes and her lips trembled. She strained her ears, her restless mind wandered until— what was that? She heard soft, stealth footsteps of someone walking towards the grove, he was careful not to crack any twig or crush any leaf beneath his feet. He reached the grove and threw himself down and dug his fingers in the ground. In the dark he plunged desperately for the bundle, half way along, his feet suddenly felt as if they rested on some icy, slippery ground. His stumbled over it in his haste and fell with a thud. A chill hush came upon Gayatri as she heard a whirring-hissing sound coming from the back of her house.

Through the crack of her window she saw the snake uncoiling itself. It stared at the intruder ready to strike, the end of its tail vibrating quickly. She jumped up wringing her hands, became agitated and stood still in painful suspense. A pang of terror ran through her, followed by a sudden overwhelming feeling of repentance.

When the first pale light of dawn appeared, Gayatri came out of her house. She saw a small crowd of bystanders at the back of her house. She hurriedly went to see the reason of the commotion. There she found her son's lifeless body sprawled under the tree, white froth trickling from the mouth of his bluish face.

In despair as she flung herself on him throwing her arms around him, holding him tight. She slowly put her son's head upon her lap gazing at him with bewildered and reproachful eyes.

Suspicions propped up when Gayatri showed mixed emotions on her son's death. At one moment she wailed for days, but again she was calm and quiet expressing a sign of relief. Rumor went around that she could be the cause of her son's death. But the villagers thought it was ludicrous and stopped worrying about the old woman. The snake charmer and his cobra vanished, and the villagers never saw or heard about them again.

With Ramkant gone, her daughter-in-law left, too, so Gayatri had no choice but to continue to take care of her small store on her own.

Over the years, all that remained of the grocery store

was a ramshackle wood and asbestos structure. But it was still holding up because of a frail old woman who still catered to the needs of the villagers for some small, insignificant items. She still went to the market to buy them and sell them again for a meagre profit, just enough to allow her to get by. Next to the store there was a little decayed thatched hut, which although, unfit for human habitation, Gayatri, bent with age, sorrow and poverty, had no choice but to live.

To the villagers, she sometimes appeared to be a strange person and her wayward behavior awed them all. The very mention of her name was enough to scare the children. She would sometimes wander for days together, heedless to weather conditions. And at other times, for no apparent reason, she hurried with light, quick steps, gazing intently at some nonspecific object, walked about the streets muttering in a very hushed tone, a few low indistinct words: "I got rid of all of them, one by one, three generations of the *gamblers of Shantipur.*"

THE BURDEN OF A WIDOW

SAROJINI WAS WIDOWED when she was in her late twenties, but sixty years of her life could not erase the glory of her beauty. She was endowed with a beautiful oval face with chiseled cut features. And her skin still retained its youthful glow because of her one and only luxury, and that was to massage herself regularly with mustard oil prior to her bath. She also used a highly odorous oil on her hair, the smell lingered on her for days, leaving it on clothes and belongings in her room.

Wasn't she the same Sarojini who wore jewelry and dressed up in fine silks when she was a young bride? The same person who anointed her hair with perfumed oil when she was the young wife of the reputed lawyer? She still looked elegant and beautiful in her white sari of widowhood. And where once a red vermillion dot, sanctifying her marriage, adorned her forehead, she now drew a long *tilak* made of sandalwood paste, extending to her nose.

Her hair, close cropped with streaks of grey in them, remained covered most of the time with the end of her sari. Her eyeglasses, round with metallic frames, only came of use when she read chapters from the sacred book *Gita* before dawn, for absolution from her mortal sins. In her hand, she held a *rudraksha mala*, a rosary strung with 109 beads, to keep track of the count of mantra repetitions. Holding the rosary in her right hand, she would use her thumb to "count" each chant by touching the bead, and then lightly pulling the bead towards her on completion of the *mantra*, moving to the next bead. Her mind would wander off sometimes during her chanting.

She tried to maintain her aloofness, but from time to time she made her presence felt everywhere and in everything unintentionally. Her unsolicited interference and comments were tolerated when she came to stay with her relatives because of the large sum of money she inherited from her husband.

The *burden of a widow* was that of rigorous abstention. Regarding touching or cooking non-vegetarian items, a corner of the sprawling kitchen was set aside for her where she could only cook her own food using separate utensils and spices. She maintained a strict vegetarian diet and any food that may have traces of paraphernalia were kept aside for the fear of contamination. Onion and garlic never found a place on her plate because it would rouse her slumbering mind and sexual desires. On *Ekadashi* (the eleventh day of the lunar month), she observed strict fast and did not even drink water. She ate alone, cooked in small amounts, and had her own way of turning the vegetarian dishes into savory, mouthwatering delicacies.

She was called *Pishima* (*father's sister*). Her parents had arranged her marriage with a well reputed lawyer, a widower twice her own age. He had children by his previous marriage, a son and a daughter. Her stepson was older than she was and her stepdaughter being of the same age. After her marriage and at such a tender age, the responsibility of the entire household fell on her shoulders. She was quite capable and efficient at her household chores, happy and loved by all the members of her family.

But soon, the uncertainties of life took a different course for her. Before the mourning period of her husband's sudden demise was over, her exalted position in the entire household transformed, it was delegated to an inferior, neglectful situation. She found herself as an antagonist, a burden to the family that she once loved. It became more pronounced in the treatment her stepson and her step daughter-in-law meted out to her. On her husband's death, property and inheritance matters caused tension and strife. Her brother-in-law and her stepson came forward clamoring for the division of the property, including the house they dwelt in.

Her brother-in-law and stepson became the primary beneficiaries, her husband had not designated her the sole beneficiary, nor did he appoint her as the sole executor of the will. As a result, her brother-in-law, the stepson, and his wife conspired to deprive their bereaved stepmother of her share in the inheritance. She could only live in and use the house instead of owning it. Brought up in an environment where patriarchal dominance was the norm of the day, the astute lawyer husband of hers favored giving his property to his son, the direct lineage. He was not in favor of his wife coming into possession of the house after his death so that it did not go to his wife's relatives after her death.

Sarojini was subjected to intense physical and emotional abuse at the hands of her stepchildren so that she would become weak and despondent and would surrender all that she owned—land, property, jewelry, even her household things. The aim was to drive her into a life of abject poverty and keep all her assets for themselves.

It so happened that one day, an earnest looking middle age man approached her and started to have a serious conversation with her. He seemed to have an extensive knowledge of the feud over the partition of the deceased lawyer's family property.

"From what I perceive," he said, "your husband's family is going to put pressure on you not to claim your share of the house and will try every possible means to evict you."

She didn't want to believe it. "According to the will, one-third of the property should come to me and the other two-thirds rightfully go to my stepson."

"I suggest you surrender your legal rights to family property, so that you can have a loving relationship with your stepson," he said.

"I know what you mean," she answered with tears in her eyes.

Of course, I want a good relationship with my children. They are my children, and I never think about them in any other way. When I was married to their father, they loved me and treated me well. Now they are indifferent because I am a widow. In their attempts to deprive me of my share they are harassing and persecuting me. They are the ones to decide what I should get, how to treat me. I have no freedom to return to my parents or to my brothers, and since I have no children, I may even be sent to Ashrams in Vrindavan," she said ominously.

Seeing her vulnerable situation, he started to manipulate her with his suave manners. He did not take long to visit her at her home and those visits became more frequent claiming that he was her long-lost cousin, related on her mother's side. She became convinced more so when he narrated some anecdotes from his childhood days, his close association with her parents, when *Sarojini* was merely a little girl holding on to her mother's apron. He won her trust completely and in exchange, he made a promise to fight for her legitimate claims to her property.

Eventually, the court ruled in her favor. She was going to get her share of the house. An appraisal of the house was made, and she was granted one third of the current market price. It was now up to her whether she wanted to stay with her stepson or leave the house with the money. Her family opted to keep the house and use it for their dwelling. As a result, *Sarojini* had no roof over her head. Eventually, she came to stay with her previously unknown cousin who urged her to live with his family.

When she came to live with her newly found cousin's family, she brought her jewelry and a considerable sum of money. She was granted a very special position, an exalted status, with everyone always doting on her. But it soon became clear that her new relative had a nefarious scheme up his sleeves. He gained full access to her funds by his sweet talk and a little bit of coaxing, with the intention of cheating her out of her money. Whenever there was a major expense, he would often put a bite on her money without her knowledge.

At the time of his daughter's wedding, he asked her to part with some of her jewelry that had been gifted by her father at the time of her wedding.

"Sarojini," he pleaded, "I'm so worried about the expenses that Ritu's wedding. Gold is so expensive nowadays, and I'm at my wit's end to procure money to buy her at least one piece of jewelry. I can't send her off to her husband's house without any jewelry,"

"Oh no you don't have to worry at all, she answered. "I still have my wedding jewelry with me. She can have my heavy necklace with a matching earring that I wore at the time of my own wedding. That will be my gift to Ritu, I'll also add two bangles, that way you can save up money on buying gold. I don't have a daughter and who will wear my jewelry. Moreover, you've done so much for me!"

"My dear sister, you're a god send! I don't know how to thank you, but I'll make sure that you live comfortably here in my house. I always tell my wife and children that it's hard to find a Pishima like you, and ...you must let me know if you want anything special to eat, are you getting enough to eat? Ritu, go get a box of *sandesh* for your Pishima," he called his daughter.

Ritu went out to get a box of fresh *sandesh* for her. She had been waiting for an opportunity to talk to Pishima. "Pishima," she said, "you should leave this house and stay somewhere else. Find a place of your own, and I'll take care of you."

"How can I leave your father when he has done so much for me?"

Ritu kept quiet and refrained from saying anything to her about her conniving father. Instead she started doing research about their genealogy to find out more about their roots, distant aunts, uncles. To her dismay, she found out that her father was not related to Pishima. Just as she feared, it was all a hoax, a plan to deceive a helpless widow and to steal her money.

Over the years, *Sarojini* 's health deteriorated, and her so-called cousin used up all her money. Her cousin looked at the frail, old lady and thought to himself, "*Maybe* a change of weather would do her good, a visit to an auspicious place would uplift her spiritual being."

Later that week, Ritu went to her parents' house for a visit and found her Pishima's room empty. There was not a sound. The familiar smell of the mustard oil that always emanated from her room was gone. All her belongings were missing. The room was dark.

"Where's Pishima?" she asked her father.

"I took her to an Ashram in Vrindavan to live out the remainder of her life," he answered impassively. "That was where she belonged, and it's best that she joined other widows living the life of a *bhikharini (a beggar)* on the banks of the Yamuna. The begging will give her *moksha* and allow her to release her soul from the cycle of rebirth, cleansing her soul and the sins of her past lives. After all, wasn't it her fault what she had brought on herself! I'm now convinced that she had accumulated lot of bad karma to be deprived of her happiness."

It was hard for Ritu to believe that her own father was talking in such a manner. Her Pishima was well provided for after her husband's death, she did not have to go to an ashram to spend the rest of her life in misery!

It was an eye opener for her, too, as she began to wonder if she ever had to face a similar fate like her

Pishima's what would happen then? Would she be sent to Vrindavan too?

Ritu decided she would go to Vrindavan to find Pishima. It was hard to single her out from the crowd of other white sari clad widows who thronged the streets of Vrindavan with their begging bowls. It was a heart wrenching sight. There were girls of different age groups amongst the widows who did not deserve to be there. Pain and sadness had dulled their young faces when life still had so much to offer to them.

"Pishima, can you recognize me, I have come to see you," she said excitedly with a smile of exalted happiness once she spotted her.

"Oh Ritu, is that you? I thought you'd forgotten me, my dear child."

"Take me to your ashram, Ritu said as they walked toward the ashram that she shared with other widows. "I should have come earlier to get you, I missed you so much, and I miss your vegetable dishes that you shared with me! Come home with me. I have grown a vegetable garden for you, and you can pick fresh vegetables and I'll prepare the same dishes that you once so loved to eat."

Sarojini's eyes shone at the prospect of having a vegetable garden. Ritu helped her to get into the waiting car and tried not to look back as they drove away. Her heart ached for the other widows, particularly the child widows hoping that someday, somebody would reach out to them, too.

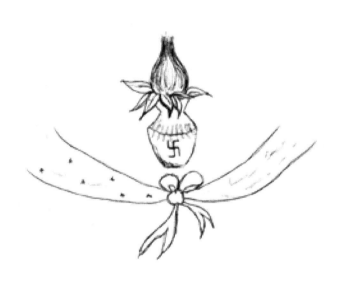

MARRIAGE MADE IN HEAVEN

APARNA'S MOTHER GAVE the good news to her husband when he came home from work, "The PhD groom from America and his family approved our daughter's picture and sent us positive feedback! They are coming to see her tomorrow!"

"Which picture did you send?" Prosoon asked enthusiastically. The recent one in her blue and gold saree or the one the Park Studio photographer took last year?"

"The pictures don't tell much. She looks ten times better than her photos! I'm sure they will say yes this time," she replied.

Suddenly, a look of gloom and hopelessness overshadowed Prosoon's face. He began to have negative thoughts about the proposal. What if nothing materialized again? His daughter had been rejected several times by a potential groom's party on account of flimsy, nonsensical reasons.

"Aparna," he called out, "why don't you brush up your Tagore songs and one of the Nazrul songs. I'm sure the groom from U.S. will love to hear some Bengali songs so that he can show you off once you go to America! They have cultural functions there also, and brides who know how to sing are much appreciated."

"Yes, father, Ma and I have already talked about it. I'll make sure the harmonium is tuned up," she said reassuringly.

Aparna was twenty-nine years old, with a postgraduate degree, fair complexion, and all the other attributes of an eligible girl. But she still remained unmarried despite her parents placing proposal ads in the matrimonial columns of the two largest newspapers in town, *The Statesman and Anandabazar Patrika*. There were hundreds of responses, but nothing clicked with her. Some of them fell short of looks, some came from different family background or were not qualified enough to make a decent living, and most asked for a huge dowry. Prosoon's contribution to the delay of his daughter's marriage had to be taken into consideration, too. Although he appeared to be a man of liberal and modern outlooks, when it came to his daughter's marriage, he was fastidious regarding her future groom's caste, background, and the degrees he had accumulated over the years. He, too, rejected prospective grooms in the process. For Aparna to marry someone of her own choice was unthinkable, so the years slipped through her fingers while she waited in anticipation to marry the right man.

The next day, the maternal uncle of Abinash, the groom, did the preliminary talk over the phone and announced the time and day of their visit to see the bride. As the time approached for the families to meet, Aparna adorned herself in an embroidered silk sari and jewelries, adding a magic glow to her fair skin. Waiting in anticipation, Aparna's parents prepared themselves with utmost care for the oncoming trial. They took care of minute details, triying to bring out the best of their mannerisms as any slip in their hospitality would ruin their daughter's prospects of getting married. And as evening slowly crept into darkness, the whole entourage of the groom's side arrived to see the bride. The entourage consisted of two unmarried sisters, the groom's cousin and his wife, and the groom himself.

Aparna on her part was calm and composed, as she had grown familiar to the ordeals of sitting and facing total strangers who would be scrutinizing her and asking random questions. It was inevitable that something unexpected would happen, and, it did. The power went off and the house went dark. Because the *Calcutta Electric Supply Board* was unable to provide power to the huge city grids, there were frequent power cuts, or what they called *load shedding*, which meant the whole city was plunged into complete darkness to save power. During that time, driven by necessity, people would turn to primitive methods of lighting up their rooms. Lamps, lanterns, and candles all became essential to bring back the light in each room that now flickered on the walls with any subtle movements. After a light knock on the door, Aparna's mother, Anamika, welcomed the groom and his family members with a lantern in her hand. The lantern with its flickering light threw shadows in the room and in the dim light Aparna stole a glance at her future husband.

On such occasions, it was customary that refreshments were offered, which consisted of large and decorated colorful sweets of various shapes and dimensions. Prosoon went out of his way to get the very best ones available in the shops.

"Please help yourself to the *rajbhogs*, they are not available in all sweet shops, I had to place a special order this morning," he insisted placing his palms together. "And please try the *patali gurer sandesh*, they are from *Mithai Bhandar* well known for their sweets for generations."

One of the unmarried sisters took a sweet and then

turned to Aparna, "Are you well-versed in *Rabindra sangeet*? If so, would you sing one for us?"

Aparna was well prepared, and she sang one of the popular songs of Rabindranath Tagore.

"It says in the paper you are a student of English literature. Tell us what books interest you most and give us your reasons for liking them," groom's cousin interrogated Aparna.

"I've read many books and the list is incredibly long. I'm afraid you will not have the patience to listen to it," Aparna answered with a smile.

Eventually, the verdict went in favor of Aparna and it was a *marriage made in heaven*. Prosoon was immeasurably impressed with the groom's degree, a PhD from NYU, and his family did not even ask for a dowry!

Regarding all Hindu marriages, the role of astrology should not be minimized. It had been said that an arranged marriage often did not materialize on grounds of mismatched zodiac signs of the proposed bride and groom. A reputed astrologer would read the astronomical chart of both the bride and the groom. If they matched, then he would tell them to go ahead with the marriage. That was the last hurdle of an arranged marriage. And, unfortunately, Aparna's horoscope did not match with Abinash's.

Needless to say, Aparna's father did not want the match to slip out of his hands, so he took the priest aside, "I would pay you any amount of money if you could come up with ideas to match the horoscope."

"No, that is impossible! You were telling me to change the course of their destiny and interfere with god's wishes!"

"But they like each other, and it will be hard for me to find a groom like him again," Prosoon, with hands folded, pleaded desperately.

At last the priest agreed to change the position of the stars and planets on the horoscopes so that they matched. No one but Prosoon and the priest knew.

The bride's parents were very pleased at the turn of events. Their daughter got married off and that too to a well-placed groom working as a professor in the US. It was beyond their expectations, so they did not hesitate to spend lavishly for their daughter's wedding. Keeping fire as the witness, she went around her husband seven times tying the knots with the man she hardly knew. The significance of circling the fire seven times meant they would remain man and wife for the next seven reincarnated lives.

The groom's family hailed from the outskirts of the city. Aparna's close encounter with her in-laws began the next day after her wedding. The train journey to the countryside was long and tiresome as she sat demurely in between her mother-in-law and her new husband. The elaborate rituals of the wedding ceremony took a toll upon Aparna. She was exhausted and overwhelmed with the sudden turn in her life. As the train tugged along, she gazed intently at the paddy fields, the black and white dots of cows in the horizon, little mud huts with thatched roofs in the far distance, filled her with sadness and a desperate longing for her parents.

It goes without saying that when you are wedded to your husband, you are wedded to the husband's family. A wife not only was an asset to the family, but an exploitable commodity handed to them. Aparna soon found herself at the beck and call of everybody. With her head lowered, partially covered with the end of her sari she would serve morning tea to her new father-in-law. She was soon entrusted with household chores. Traditionally, it was expected that a newly married bride would cook, serve, and wait upon the family, and when her turn came to eat, she was so tired that she no longer had an appetite.

Abinash, her husband did not see eye to eye with his parents' old traditions, and during his stay at his parents'

house, he made passive attempts at changing the ways of life of his family. Aparna, instead, thought otherwise. She thought of herself as being more fortunate than others. She believed that her stay with her in-laws would be a short one. Her husband, after he had returned to America to prepare a home for her, would soon send plane tickets and she would join him.

The letters he wrote to Aparna were quite regular at the beginning. She would grab the letter; conceal them in her blouse and read them in the privacy of her room. When she emerged from her room, she became aware of envious glances from her sisters-in-law. But Aparna did not feel any grudge towards them nor did she try to create any kind of estrangements with her husband's family. Instead, her heart went out to those thousands of women who have gone into obscurity, lost forever in ordinary mundane affairs of life, lived for the sake of living, or stayed married for the sake of being married. Their silent tears were never seen as they were wiped off with corners of their sarees hurriedly. One of Abinash's brothers came home after a hard day's work and did not even ask his wife whether she was alright, let alone listen to her grievances. The brother's wife would go to bed softly lest she wake up the whole household, even more exhausted than her husband. The blissful act of love turned into an abrupt, loveless, matter of fact performance.

Aparna soon found herself trapped within her husband's family. She waited expectantly for another letter from her husband, but nothing came for a week, which then turned into a month. She forced herself to believe that he might be busy or that he was having a difficult time finding the right house for her. In her mind she tried to justify his silence, frantically looking for an explanation for her abandonment.

"How come Abinash has stopped writing to me?" She asked one of his sisters.

"This is the busiest time of the year," the sister said. "He could be loaded up with his course work."

Aparna thought it wise to leave her husband's house and visit her parents for a while, so she soon left for Kolkata. Once at her father's house she began to relax and stopped worrying about her husband. One day, during the last vestiges of spring, Aparna went with her mother to shop for the occasion of the beginning of Bengali New Year. It was at one of the sari shops that she bumped into a small thin Caucasian woman who appeared to have come for a visit from the U.S, attempting to barter with the shopkeeper in a loud American accent. Aparna and the American woman soon fell into a conversation.

"Which part of the country are you from?" Aparna asked.

"I live in New York in America. My husband teaches at NYU," the woman replied.

Aparna's heart jumped at when she heard NYU. She blurted out, "Do you know anybody by the name of Abinash Chatterjee?"

"Of course! Such a small world, I know him very well," she answered surprisingly. "I'm very good friends with his wife, Nancy! They just had their first child! Are you a friend of theirs?"

Aparna's face turned ghostly, and she couldn't believe what she heard. "No, ah … yes … he visited here once, but I'm afraid I'm in a hurry," Aparna quickly turned away before the other woman could see the tears begin to swell in her eyes. Aparna hurried out of the shop. She felt as though everything around her was revolving and that the Earth began moving under her feet, like an earthquake. In the street, she held on to her mother's arm and didn't look back.

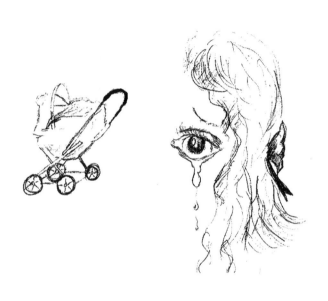

THE BASHING OF
THE HUSBANDS

SEEMA LOOKED FORWARD to her tenth wedding anniversary party at her sprawling house in Oakhurst Estates. She, along with her husband, Mahendra, recently moved to their estate just few months back and were eager to establish their status as the proud owner of their marvelous house.

The house had a panoramic view of a grassy green meadow with rolling hills, dotted with wild shrubs of blooming flowers adding color to the distant horizon. An enormous oak tree near the house would cast a deep shadow which engulfed its surroundings, protecting the much of the backyard from the harsh daylight sun. Here in the shade, the white striped chipmunks and tufted squirrels with their long, bushy tails darted back and forth gathering ripe acorns from the ground as sparrows chirped melodiously from within the branches. The scenic beauty was one of the special features of the house, and this spectacular view could be seen from every window. White, pink, and red oleanders concealed part of the front porch adding beauty to the gravel path lined with olive trees, which was often trodden by an occacional family of deer. At night, the animal kingdom in the far distance stirred as evidenced by the coyotes howling in the darkness.

It was a perfect house for the upcoming event, yet as the evening approached, Seema's nervousness and anxiety increased even though preparations for the party progressed without any mishap. At sunset, the guests in their showy foreign-made cars pulled up into the driveway. Mahendra greeted the guests as they arrived with a big smile. Among the guests, the amiable and cheerful Srivastava couple arrived first, being punctual always. Next, came Mr. and Mrs. Roy, who were followed by the Chatterjees and the Mondols, and finally followed by Raj and Shushma. All were charmingly pleasant and agreeable—so much so that they seemed to compete with one another to see who could be the most entertaining. Lastly, the door opened again and Mahendra escorted in Mita, a single woman in her forties, who joined the other ladies. The evening went along quite smoothly and pleasantly.

After the nine-course meal, it was as if by an unspoken law of nature that the gentlemen seated themselves in a room away from their womenfolk, who in all their fineries made themselves comfortable in one of the adjoining rooms. The men, by nature, refrained from talking about their wives as such domestic issues did not mix well with their world of games, politics, investments where they showed off their ample knowledge. The women, however, needed privacy because they talked about anything and everything, admiring one another's outfit, jewelries, arguing about school systems, and tried to keep abreast with all the happenings around the world. They were fond of updating the movies one must see, the latest fashions, places to visit, spiced up with the narration about the achievements of their multi-talented children, each trying to establish the fact of being one step ahead of the other.

Satiated and relaxed, the ladies invariably hit upon their favorite topic: *bashing of the husbands*. This conversation unraveled the truth about the faults and failures of their husbands causing displeasure and constraint on their marital relationship. A discussion, that gave the ladies a feeling of camaraderie, a spirit of conviviality. Mrs. Roy, a woman with a small plump oval face, worked as a financial analyst with a highly renowned company started the bashing. "Pijush does not lift a finger on household chores," she blurted out, inviting others to join in the conversation. "With a full-time job and managing the home front, I get stressed out at the end of the day".

Mrs. Srivastava, inspired by Mrs. Roy's rhetoric outbursts decided to play her part. "At least your husband is not an ill-tempered man who gets angry easily. My husband is a time bomb ready to explode with a little spark."

"Why, what happened?" Mrs. Roy asked.

Mrs. Srivastava had a tendency of repeating herself when she was emotional and now tears welled up in her eyes. "The other day... the other day, it slipped my mind to deposit a check in the bank, and he was so furious that he flung a glass jar of melted butter on the kitchen floor. The floor was filled with thousand pieces of broken glasses. I was in no shape to tell my boss why I was late for work."

Chandita Chatterjee, who had a photographic memory, was endowed with an extraordinary talent and habit of narrating events in her life in a grandiose scale. "When I first came to United States, I was like a fish out of water, my husband never bothered to enlighten me with the ways of life in a new, unknown country. I was left entirely on my own. I begged him to give me driving lessons, which he did eventually, but always ended up in fights."

"Why didn't you go to a driving school? That could have solved your problem," Mrs. Mondol said sympathetically.

"He thought I would never pass driving tests, according to him it was a complete waste of money and effort," said Chandita who eventually got her license after three attempts. However, Chandita wasn't done complaining. "When my husband came home at night, I used to serve food on the table and then disappear from the kitchen. When I would return to clean up, yellow stains of turmeric on the tablecloth borne witness to his frenzies along with half the *daal* and rice was left on the floor. He must have used the dinner plate like a frisbee when he ate." The women roared with laughter.

Mahendra interrupted the ladies and asked, "Can I offer any of you ladies some chai this evening?"

Several of the ladies raised their hands with big flirtatious eyes staring at the charming gesture.

"Oh, I wish my husband was more like Mahendra. He's so kind and thoughtful. Where did you find such a kind hearted husband, Seema?" Sushma asked poutingly.

Seema ignored all the comments and smiled. She brought in sweets and served them but abstained from any of the conversations.

Aruna Mondol, a doctor by profession, picked up the thread of the conversation. "My husband constantly reminded me to look for a job as soon as I came to this country. He was more worried about the procurement of college fees. Instead of enjoying our newborn baby girl, he was concerned about her future."

"You know what Raj did?" Shushma joined in with her complains. "Raj always made a fuss about my appearance; he did not hesitate to go through my wardrobe to select what I should wear to parties."

"Well you can interpret that in two ways," said Mrs. Saha, who was a science teacher in the local middle school. "Either he cares for you too much or he is controlling your life." Mrs. Saha was an excellent cook, but her husband did not appreciate her. Not a word of encouragement was ever given, and he always looked dispassionately at the food she prepared. So, she looked to her friends for compliments.

"For everyone who is unhappy, it's time to hit the road," Mita said. She was a twice- divorced accountant, who looked at all the ladies and smiled disdainfully. "As far as I am concerned, there is no room for adjustments, I walked out of two failed marriages unscathed. I will not allow anybody to ruin my life," she said triumphantly. "You should have left your spouses a long time ago."

Seema parted her lips to say a few words, but suddenly Mahendra made his appearance and laid a gentle hand on her shoulder, drawing her toward him. It was an affectionate gesture leaving no room for doubt that they were a happy couple who adored each other. Unlike other ladies, she was too timid to share a remark or an opinion of her own.

Seema hardly slept the night of the party. The stories told by her friends—and her exhaustion from all the preparations—contributed to her restless night. She looked back at the ten years of her wedded life with a new awakening. The lights of her life turned off when she discovered that her husband Mahendra did not want to raise any children. He believed that bringing a child into the world meant too many responsibilities. Seema, on the other hand, dreamed of having children since she was a little girl. Every time she brought up the subject of having kids, Mahendra would stay firmly with his decision and brush it aside.

The worst part was that Seema had been pregnant twice in the past ten years, but Mahendra's harsh demands ultimately would result in no conceived children. On both occasions, when she was overjoyed to tell him about the pregnancy and his reconsideration, his personality changed overnight, and he became irrational, threatening to leave the marriage, thus putting enormous burden on her to make the decision to terminate both pregnancies.

Eventually autumn crept in and painted the landscape with its golden hue, announcing the approach of winter. Seema, to her utter joy, discovered she was pregnant again. But her happiness was overshadowed by her fears of Mahendra's wishes. Seema kept the news a secret from her husband, who failed to notice any profound change in his wife's physical appearance. Seema's frail frame and loose clothes enabled her to conceal the pregnancy.

It turned out that Seema had an aunt, a distant relative who had lived in California for many years. She soon started making contacts with her aunt who was thrilled at the idea of having a niece and the aunt soon planned to visit Seema. Mahendra failed to detect anything unusual from his wife's over enthusiastic welcome to her relatives, about whom she hardly even mentioned before. Seema befriended her aunt during her stay and confided in her about her situation and her predicament.

Kusum, her aunt, was the embodiment of all goodness in a human being. She did not have children, so there was an emptiness in her life too, longing for someone on whom she could bestow her unconditional love. Seema decided to spend time in California with her aunt's home once her pregnancy was no longer possible to keep hidden, with plans to have the baby there without Mahendra's knowledge. Unfortunately, her aunt thought it otherwise.

"I think you must go back to your husband and have the baby with him, my child," she said and decided to send her back home assuring her that Mahendra eventually would welcome the baby once it was born.

Seema finally agreed to go back and face her husband, regardless of the consequences. But the very next morning, while Seema was in the shower, Kusum heard a piercing scream. She knocked at the door, found Seema standing in a massive pool of blood. Seema had a miscarriage. It was a dramatic and unexpected ending to her dream of being a mother and to the promise of a more fulfilled life.

Seema was taken to the hospital immediately who ultimately contacted Mahendra giving him the news that she was pregnant. In the light of her history from her previous terminations, the doctors described that much scarring and irreversible changes to her reproductive organs would prevent her from conceiving naturally from now on. Seema would become barren.

Another year went by, a New Year's Eve party was to be held at Chandita's house. The same guests that were at Seema's tenth wedding anniversary had gathered on that day, and again the ladies seated themselves in comfortable places ready to converse, argue, and share new narrations from their books of everyday life.

This year, Seema was the first to open the conversation. For the first time in ten years, Seema opened the flood gates and described the hidden side of Mahendra, her history of three failed pregnancies, and his rigid and unyielding stand of not having any children. The other ladies' eyes were all glued to Seema, mouths dropped attempting to empathize with her. Seema would give the biggest bashing of her husband that the ladies heard in a very long time.

A BITTER TASTE

"YOU GOT UP EARLY today and finished your morning chores?" Asharani's sister-in-law asked surprisingly. "You look excited. What's the matter?"

"Don't tell anybody yet, Kamini, but Roopam sent a plane ticket for me. He wants me to go to America and visit him. It's been seven years he left and now he wants me to spend time with his daughter whom I didn't get the chance to hold. I cry every night before I go to bed, and I also miss Madhavi my daughter-in-law! But I am afraid everybody will dislike the idea and encourage me not to go."

"Of course, you'll go! Nobody is going to stop you, I assure you," Kamini answered.

That summer afternoon when the blistering heat of long summer months made its way through the streets of Kolkata, a feeling of drowsiness was in the air after a midday sumptuous meal. The necessity of afternoon sicstas forced the shops to bring their shutters down at noon for an interim period. And it was during those hours when the extended family members of her ancestral home were lazing on the mats that Asharani stepped out of her house to take a long flight overseas.

Wrapped only in an ordinary sari and with her hair twisted up into a casual bun, she was far from being a modern, sophisticated woman. At first, she appeared to be intimidated by her unfamiliar surroundings at the airport, looked furtively for a place to sit and deposit her luggage close to her legs. Moreover, in case she got cold on the plane, she carried a red, hand woven cotton shawl woven with a spray of iridescent colors. And every now and then she took out a picture of a little girl, standing demurely with her parents. She gazed longingly at the photo of her grandchild, held it to her bosom for an instant, and then looked around to make sure nobody was watching her. Then she hurriedly put the photo back into her big purse with her other personal things.

As she was waited to be called to board the international flight, every vein in her body was filled with excitement with the thought of seeing her son's daughter first and foremost in her mind. Soon, though, doubts surged up and she thought of getting out of the airport to run back where she belonged. But there was no going back. Roopam wanted her to go, and so she was on her way.

As a matter of fact, Asharani had never been outside Kolkata. She was one of the many children of a well-known family where tradition was paramount. Her relatives had mixed feelings regarding her trip, too. Sometimes they thought she was lucky to be able to cross the sea, but other times they were apprehensive about the uncertainties that lay ahead.

Her friends, neighbors, and well-wishers who visited to bid her bon voyage were worried for her. Some predicted Asharani would undergo a complete metamorphosis.

"I can't wait to see Asharani when she comes back," one of her good friends said. "She is going to change a lot. Maybe she'll refuse to talk to us, or she'll pick up an American accent and forget her own mother tongue!"

Another friend said, "Are you going to wear pants once you go there? I heard that saris are cumbersome in winter. I can see you in jeans, high heels, and perhaps even driving a car, too!"

While waiting to board the flight, her thoughts turned towards her son and her daughter-in-law. Is he the same

Roopam whom she sent abroad to pursue his studies? Tears of happiness welled up in her eyes at the coming reunion with her son and his family. She hoped he would be kind towards her and would take care for her just like before.

Even though Roopam was raised in an extended family, there was always a special bond between him and his mother, and this was more so as he lost his father at quite an early age. His mother meant everything to Roopam, he was always bright and well-mannered and left no room for others to dislike him for any reason.

Every year, at the end of the final exams he would show his report card to his mother first saying, "Look mother, I got an A in all subjects," which would bring a smile to her face, opening up an avenue of dreams of the distant future.

As she thought about her son, she began to cry and then to worry about her appearance. Her fingers went up to her hair, which she thought was too oily, and she worried about not being able to converse in English except for very few words that she learnt from a Bengali to English language translation book. Her efforts at translating Bengali to English often resulted in a very different meaning far from what she actually wanted to say. As she worried, the final call for boarding the plane was announced and she took a seat on the plane.

In due time, Asharani reached her destination. She was greeted by a jean clad, short haired, young woman in her early thirties. Apart from her name, Madhavi, she stood before her as an embodiment of a totally transformed Bengali bride. She remembered welcoming her son's new bride with blowing conch shells, ritual ululations, her right foot immersed in a plate of milk with *alta*, a red dye, as she entered her house. And she remembered that after the ceremonial welcoming of the bride Madhavi took upon the chores and responsibilities of her new family as expected. She tried to please everybody, in every possible way to fulfill the expectations of her family, to be an ideal daughter-in-law.

Madhavi rose early in the morning, made ablutions in cold water, put vermilion in the mid parting of her hair, and a red dot on her forehead, as was the custom. She prepared herself to do the different rituals involving different deities of the worship room by offering flowers picked from the garden, the incense sticks to burn, and mantras to chant for the well-being of the family. She spent her entire morning in the preparation of family meals, starting with tea, then an elaborate breakfast. Her head covered with the end of her sari she served tea and snacks to her mother-in-law, then other members of the family, who tend to wake up at different intervals. When food was prepared and eaten, nobody cared to ask if anything was left for the new bride.

For her part, Madhavi felt that her life was nothing short of the life of a maid in the garb of a bride. Roopam did not involve himself in the mundane, daily happenings of life. At the end of the day fatigue and exhaustion overcame her. She crept into her bed stealthily lest she wake up the family only to find Roopam in deep sleep. She was was overjoyed when Roopam brought her with him to a new country, away from tradition-bound, age-old customs to a land of endless opportunities, unlimited freedom. So, she welcomed her mother-in-law in her newly acquired social etiquettes, it was not unbecoming on her part.

Asharani knew that change was inevitable and that her daughter-in-law's transformation did not come abruptly but rather over the years. When Madhavi did not bow down and touch her feet to show honor and respect, instead bringing her palms together in a symbolic gesture, a gesture unthinkable for Asharani, she swallowed her pride and put the blame on western culture. After all, why would she jeopardize her relationship with her son and the risk the opportunity of seeing her only granddaughter over such trivial matters.

"*The whole reason I have come here*," she told herself, "is *to shower them with my love and affection, not to criticize them.*"

After preliminary exchange of warm embraces and the drive from the airport, Asharani stepped into her son's sprawling house.

"Ma you're going to like it here, I promise. You don't have to worry about anything,"

Roopam assured his mother enthusiastically. "You will play with Mimi all day long, educate her with Bengali culture and teach her a few Bengali words. A bonding between you and your granddaughter will be the best thing in the world. Madhavi and I always wanted Mimi to know her grandmother well."

Roopam took his mother to the east side of the house to show her room and put her belongings in one corner. Asharani had never been to a large and luxurious home with all the amenities of a modern life. Little did she realize that she was surrounded by high-tech gadgets and appliances that would confuse her terribly.

First of all, the idea of having her saris on hangers in a closet was completely unknown to her so her eyes searched for a wooden rack where she could keep her daily wear clothes. She looked at the carpeted floor and longed for her concrete courtyard and tiled floor back home.

It was a common knowledge that Asharani had OCD. Madhavi remembered how her mother-in-law washed her hands and feet frequently even though they were clean. The clothes that were hung outside for the sun to dry were rewashed if she detected a speck of dirt in them.

The most horrifying experience of her stay was undeniably the whole process of using the bathroom. She fumbled with the shower knob, could never adjust the right temperature of the water. Although her son introduced her to all the gadgets of the house, it was hard for her to grasp everything in such a short time. She began to fuss about her sarees coming out crinkled from the dryer, so she started looking for a clothesline so that she could air dry her clothes. Asharani thought about the family Dhobi who would come to collect the soiled clothes to be washed and ironed.

At night Madhavi whispered to Roopam. "Do you think it was a good idea to bring your mother here? I think it's hard for her to get used to our way of life.

"Don't you worry," he said. "She'll learn fast."

When Asharani was asked to chop vegetables, she was not used to the chopping board, back home she used a *boti*, and squatted on the ground to cut the vegetables along the sharp edge of the knife while balancing the wooden stand with her toe. And although Roopam subscribed to

Dish network, so that his mother could watch her favorite shows on TV, Asharani couldn't figure out how to use the three remote control devices lying on the coffee table.

Needless to say, Madhavi did not see eye to eye with her mother-in-law over a lot of things, and her imperiousness and *bitter taste* of disdain did not take long to reveal itself. Could it be the reason of her going through all the hardships she had to face when she came as a newly wedded bride? Asharani's way of doing things displeased her, and as time passed, Madhavi became less tolerant and more impatient and irritable towards her mother-in-law.

There was no doubt that Asharani loved to cook for her son, and she enjoyed preparing all his favorite dishes that he enjoyed as a little boy. It was of such immense pleasure to stand next to her son, watching him relishing the food she prepared. But Roopam's innocent compliments about her mother's cooking began to cause a rift between the young couple.

One evening, the rift turned into an argument. "All these years who cooked for you? Where was your mother at that time?" Madhavi said, trying not to cry. "You never appreciate what I do for you anymore. You've changed a lot ever since your mother came here.

"Where is this coming from Madhavi?" Roopam asked. "Why do you get so upset over such simple things?

I was simply being nice to her after she came all the way to be with us. She wanted to go back to the days we had left behind, and I was appreciative, that's all. Will you act in that manner if your own mother is trying to be nice to me?"

But the matter did not end there. The next day, Madhavi entered the kitchen and began to cut vegetables. When her mother-in-law entered the kitchen, she said, "Ma, why don't you lie down and let me cook today. You've been cooking ever since you came here, and now it's my turn to cook for you. Don't you want to taste your daughter-in-law's dishes?" In this ingenious way, Madhavi stripped her mother-in-law from the chores she loved.

But cooking was not the only problem. Whenever Madhavi saw her own daughter, Mimi, cuddling up next to her grandmother, a spark of jealousy ignited within her. She feared Mimi would become too attached to her grandmother and jeopardize her position as her mother. Soon she began to look for pretexts to sever the closeness between them.

"Clean up your room, put away the toys, and get ready for bath," Madhavi said to Mimi. "Remember, you have school tomorrow," she would tell Mimi after dinner. At first Asharani did not pay much heed to these changes of behavior, she would even nudge Mimi and tell her to listen to her mother and finish her chores. But, after a while it dawned on her that she had been denied the opportunity to do the things she loved. She was not needed, and the feeling that she was not wanted began to hurt.

She noticed the small disagreements between her son and his wife, and Asharani tried to de-escalate the growing conflict before they spiraled out of control. She began to fear that such damaging outbursts would result in a breakup of their marriage. She thought of resolving things between them by minimizing the issues of conflict.

Winter months slowly crept in bringing with it the harsh cold of the season. Asharani preferred to stay inside and the thought of going back where she belonged was uppermost in her restless mind. Finally, one day she approached her son.

"Roopam," she said, "I've been thinking a lot about this matter my son, and now that winter is here, I don't want to get sick and be a burden to you and Madhavi. You know how exorbitantly high the doctor's fees are in this country. I think it will be a good idea to go back home before it gets too cold."

"But Ma, you just came! Roopam protested. "It's hardly a couple of months, and you'll enjoy everything more once the winter is gone. Moreover, Mimi is going to miss you.

Who is going to tell her the tales from *Ramayana* and *Mahabharata*? She even wrote a short paragraph about her grandma's visit for her school."

"I understand. Don't you think I'm going to miss her, too? She is the reason I came all the way, just to be with her. But they need me at home too, Kamini broke her hand, and she is insisting on my going back. It's hard for her to manage everything when her hand is in slings."

All right, Ma, as you wish. I will make Mimi understand," Roopam assured his mother.

"We are on the last chapters of *Ramayana*, and I will finish it before I leave," Asharani said as she wiped tears away before Roopam noticed. "You must come with your family sometimes, people at home want to see your little daughter, too."

At last, amidst tears and goodbyes, the day arrived when Asharani boarded the plane for her return journey. She was welcomed home by her relatives and friends with jubilation, and she realized that she was missed. Her friends and family were surprised to see that she had not changed a bit, contrary to their fears and apprehensions.

Often, she would narrate experiences of her short stay over cups of teas in the evenings. Sometimes she appeared to be sad, and at other times, she was happy about the fact that she was with her son for a brief period of time. The discomforts she had faced were nothing in comparison to the fact that she was able to feed her son special dishes.

Her friends listened to the anecdotes intently so much so that, the same stories told over and over became distorted and fictitious, losing their relevance. But Asharani was always very careful to leave out one aspect of her story. She did not talk about Madhavi's overbearing behavior towards her because she loved her son so much.

MISTAKES OF THE PAST

THE SEDUCTIVE, SULTRY, heavily scented fragrance of tubular roses filled the night air. No wonder it was called the *Fragrance of the Night*. Accompanying it, a subtle aroma of jasmine and rose promised a romantic night for the newlyweds.

It was Shimonti's first night after the wedding and the womenfolk of the house prepared her for the special night. She was bedecked with flowers, not an inch of her body was unadorned. Her nuptial bed was beautifully decorated with strings of Jasmine flowers entwined on the four bedposts. Rose petals were strewn all over the embroidered bedspread and on the floor. The ladies ushered her into her chamber, giggling, bursting with excitement as they had been waiting eagerly to bear witness to this moment of conjugal bliss.

She looked around the bedroom with uncertainty. The heat began to suffocate her too and she began to feel shaky and light headed after the elaborate wedding rituals. She climbed into bed and drew her knees up to her chin in a fetal position. She shivered at the thought of being in the same room with a total stranger. This was not the wedding night she had dreamed of, and she felt like a sacrificial lamb readied and prepared for a devouring monster.

Her husband stepped into the room. He had his hand on the door knob. He turned it quietly, pushed the door shut and peeked in the dim light of the bedroom. Shimonti jumped and gathered up her clothes to cover her feet, twisting the end of her sari in nervousness.

The lamp on the bedside table illuminated the room with a soft romantic glow casting a shadow on Shimonti's veiled face. He came towards her, closer to where she sat with knees drawn up, surrounded by red and white rose petals, some crushed, withered and curled up as the weight of her body fell on them. In the dim light, Anoop partially lifted the veil from the face of his bride. He then slowly removed the flowers that were entwined with the veil, and her face came into full view. He was looking at a beautiful but an anxious face, visibly shaken. But he was enchanted.

"Are you cold?" he asked.

She lost her voice as she nodded her head. She was frozen with fear.

"There is nothing to be afraid of my dear."

He sat down next to her on the bed. He gazed at her without taking his eyes off of her, turned her face towards him, gently kissed her soft lips, and caressed her hair with his fingers. Her face turned crimson not daring to look up, goose bumps appeared on her skin in fear, and her toes curled up as she drew them underneath her sari when Anoop moved nearer to kiss her again. He was a man of gentle ways and was not disappointed for not having an incredible wedding night. He thought that his wife, with her upbringing and modesty would want to wait for his advances in resigned passiveness. Moreover, he had no intention to be hasty.

"I know you are tired. You should get some rest. All these days of wedding rituals have surely worn you out," he said with a yawn. "I myself can barely stay awake, and we have our whole lives ahead of us. Tonight need not be any different, we will surely make it up, take rest, and sleep off the night."

Anoop took off his formal wedding attire, climbed into bed, and turned over on his back. Shimonti's too turned over onto her back and straitened her body. But she could not sleep. An unknown fear and tension began to build up within her.

"I think we should talk," she whispered. "I have something to tell you, and I don't know how to s a y i t . No one would listen to me. My parents tell me that marriage will be the best thing for me. But I don't want to hurt your feelings. Please do not hate me, it's not my fault."

She apprehensively put her hand on his arm.

"Let's talk about it tomorrow," he answered disinterestedly.

Early next morning, Shimonti was in the kitchen to prepare breakfast for both of them when Anoop walked in and gave her a hug and planted a kiss on her cheek.

"What was it that you wanted to tell me last night my beloved?" drawing her close as he asked.

Her face turned pale and lost its color at the mention of the secret that she tried hard to unlock the previous night. She began with an evasive answer, not knowing how to talk about the matter nonchalantly. But her husband's soothing words helped her to talk about the matter that had been bothering her since her parents agreed she should marry him. She smiled at him.

He noticed a ton of pain hidden behind her smile. "It's okay if you want to discuss it later, you know."

But she blurted it out as if she were midway through a conversation with herself. "How could I do this? You should have gotten yourself a perfect wife who is unscathed. I pleaded with my parents, but they did not listen. I will do anything in the world to make you happy, please do not hate me."

"Look, my dear, whatever it was, let's put everything behind. If what you want to tell me is so painful to you, then don't try to say it. Don't torment yourself by telling me about your past life, I don't need any explanations." He left the kitchen and moments later she heard the main door shut. She walked over to the table and picked up his untouched breakfast.

At night, Anoop was in bed, head propped up against a pillow, reading the newspaper. He soon folded the paper and put it by the bedside. He removed his glasses and scanned the room looking for his wife. She was not there. He found her sitting in the living room next to the lampshade reading a two- year old edition of a magazine on architecture. He told her that he could sleep on the sofa and she could have the bed—just to show that he saw through her act and knew she would not join him in the bedroom. That night as she lay on her side, the strange and insidious pantomime of images and sounds that she often saw in her dreams, kept coming back to her. However hard she tried to erase the memory of the unpleasant things that occurred on that fateful day, they seemed to rush back turning her life into a miserable one.

It was May, and Shimonti's family took a much-desired trip to Darjeeling, a cooler hilly spot in West Bengal. She opted to stay back to finish up with her summer courses so she could graduate on time. But during one of those lazy afternoons, Narendra came calling. He was a distant cousin, and about a decade older than Shimonti. And he was married.

She knew him for a long time and had no inhibitions in asking him to step inside the house. He was teaching math to undergraduate students at a local college, and Shimonti asked if he could help her with her math which she found hard to cope with. He was quite enthusiastic and became a frequent visitor to her house. She prepared tea and snacks regularly in anticipation of his visits and he made sure they did not go to waste.

In between math lessons they would hit upon other topics and talk for long hours. He would relate stories of his students while she would narrate stories about her friends in college, about teachers and their boring lectures.

One afternoon, Narendra did not turn up, and Shimonti sat beside the door all evening, worried about him, until she stood up to prepare dinner. From kitchen she could hear a loud banging on the door, Shimonti opened the door to find Narendra visibly inebriated. He stumbled inside and tried to hold a normal conversation for a little while. Shimonti, seeing him in this condition started to stay away from him. But Narendra's strong hands easily reached out and grabbed her, he pulled her towards him. There was no one around and she began to feel very unsafe.

She squirmed and tried to move away again, but he laughed at her foolishness and held her tightly. His hands seemed to be everywhere sinking into her soft flesh, his unshaved cheeks chafing against her skin. She struggled to get him off, putting up a strong fight, but he was too strong for her as he forced himself on her. In a split second her world was upside down, was overwhelmed with utmost shame and fear, and regretted being in the same room with a man in an empty house.

She had known Narendra most of her life and had great respect for him and his wife, Sanchita. How was she going to confront them ever again when she felt as though it was her mistake to have him in the house? She felt miserable about it.

The fear of abandonment by her family and friends strongly warned her from confiding to anybody. It became torturous and painful to be in the same room with Narendra whenever he came for family gatherings. Her tormentor on the contrary, carried on like nothing had happened. She had difficulty letting go of a time in her life that greatly upset her emotional well-being. Shimonti yearned for some support and not being able to tell anyone, she began to isolate herself and became a total recluse. Anger replaced remorse and she thought she needed to tell someone. She attempted to confront Sanchita, Narendra's wife.

"Do you love Narendra a lot?" She asked her out of context.

Sanchita giggled at the oddity of the question. "Why did you want to know that? Suddenly you want to know about my love life. Get a life for yourself, Shimonti."

"I was just curious," Shimonti said.

Shimonti could not bring up the subject thinking it would ruin their relationship.

In the meantime, Shimonti finished her degree, and when the question of marriage came up, she declined vehemently. Her lack of interest in finding a husband for herself resulted in the postponement of her marriage. But after three years, she broke her silence and confided to her mother whose initial reaction was anger towards her for withholding the matter from her knowledge. Then her mother accused her for not being wise enough to thwart a man's advances.

"Whatever happened that evening should be kept in deep secrecy." She said. "You should never tell anyone. Not even your husband."

When Anoop came with the marriage proposal for Shimonti, it was accepted without much ado, even though Anoop had been previously married, but now divorced. The two were married quickly amidst pomp and splendor and accompanied with a grand reception.

Anoop was patient with his new wife, but after a week or so after the wedding night, he asked, "What did you mean you were not perfect, Shimonti?"

Anoop's gentle and comforting words encouraged her to unburden her secret. She told him everything she kept inside and how wrong it was for Narendra to take advantage of her.

"That was in the past my dear," Anoop, always forgiving, took his wife in his arms to reassure her.

One Sunday morning, Shimonti and Anoop went to surprise her parents by visiting them. When they arrived, Narendra and Sanchita happen to be there visiting as well. Despite making attempts to avoid communication and contact, Shimonti's mother was, reluctantly, forced to introduce them to each other. She was wise to not have invited Narendra and his wife to her daughter's wedding; she wanted to protect her from any painful feelings on such a joyous occasion.

Narendra who was sitting in the living room introduced himself to Anoop. Anoop did not reply back. Instead, he slapped Narenda with his open palm full across the face. Narenda rocked back and then steadied himself, blinking, Anoop stuck a finger in Narenda's face.

"This was long overdue. You are a scoundrel, and if I ever catch you so much as looking in my wife's direction, I will kill you," he threatened.

Narendra's wife, Sanchita, ran into the room from the kitchen on hearing the commotion and saw the two men glaring at each other. She looked at Anoop and immediately recognized him. Anoop turned and saw Sanchita, flabbergasted, dropped his hands and appeared ghostly pale. From the way they looked at each other, it was not hard for Shimonti to discern that both Anoop and Sanchita knew each other.

Shimonti took Anoop's hand and left her parent's home. The got into the car and Anoop still staggered at the entire encounter, had difficulty saying any words. As they reached the outskirts of the town, he finally spoke.

"With regard to *mistakes of the past*, Shimonti, I have to say that I am not perfect either."

Shimonti looked up at her husband.

"I never told you about my previous marriage. I was married to Sanchita long time back. She left me because I too had cheated on her."

Shimonti stared outside the open window at the countryside, letting him tell his entire story of his failed and adulterated marriage. As the streets of Kolkata began to disappear, the city skyline looked fresh and clean from afar after the monsoon rain; but the cold, refreshing breeze on her face did not exhilarate her. She thought about rolling up the window but left it open. For her, the summer days now seemed lackluster. The rest of Anoop's words dissolved in the cold, wet wind that blew into her face. It was going to be a long ride back home.

A LITTLE BIT OF
YESTERDAY

WHEN DEBORATI WAS notified about her twentieth college reunion, she thought of the old college friends from her past whom she would have the chance to meet again. She began to speculate as to which of them would show up and which would not. Most of them might have drifted away to distant places living new lives. Some of them might have already exited from this world, but the thought of meeting her old classmates exhilarated her. Her bygone college days seemed like yesterday, full of memories both good and bad, with the exception of some that seemed so hard to erase from her memory.

It was a beautiful summer morning in Mumbai. As she had been waiting impatiently for this day, Deborati rose up early from bed to take her train ride to her old college city. The evening was already nearing when she arrived, and it was not too long before she found a place to reconnect with her old college friends with their spouses. The men all conversed about their achievements in life, and women talked about their fine houses, and bragged about the talents their children possessed. Many faces seemed familiar to her.

Deborati looked over her shoulders into the crowd in order to catch a glimpse of one face, a face that was hard to forget, enigmatic and yet strongly irresistible at once. It was of her friend Tanusree. She remembered the first time they met in college and with a rueful smile, she thought back to the days they had first met.

It was the beginning of their freshmen year at college in their dormitory cafeteria. Tanusree was the type of person who preferred to be alone, reading a book quietly in the back corner of the cafeteria. Debaroti, on the other hand, loved to make friends. She had a great personality, a fantastic sense of humor, and an eager radiant smile for all who came into contact with her.

It was Debaroti who ultimately came up to the table at the far corner occupied by none other than Tanusree whose face was glued to a book, despite the atmosphere being non-conducive for anyone to accomplish any manner of reading. "Hello, I am Debi. Do you mind if I sit with you?" she stood there with a big smile on her face.

Startled, Tanusree lifted her face from the book, "Umm, Hi, sure."

Deborati continued, "I'm trying to grab something to eat, but there is a huge line for the food. I hear they make savory chicken kabobs here. The simmering coffee of this place has its reputation, too. You can smell it all the way from the stairs. Have you ever tried coffee with kabobs?" Debaroti asked gleefully.

Tanusree shook her head.

"How about we order hot coffee and chili chicken kabobs while we get to know each other?" Debaroti asked with a bright smile again. "I hear a lot of interesting things about this cafeteria. Not only do people come here to eat and pass time, it's a cozy place to meet up and or to do joint studies. But I find it amazing as to how do they manage to concentrate with so much noise. It's unhealthy, too. The air is filled with cigarette smoke."

She breathed in a lung full, flaring her nostrils and raising her eyebrows, waving her wrists as if she was somehow ushered the air into her nose, and then exhaled vehemently with a disgusted face. "Oh, and the lights are dim and sometimes the fans don't work, thanks to power shortages. I don't' know why people like the cafeteria so much." Deborati finally paused to hear a response from Tanusree.

Tanusree, regarded the excited and inquisitive look on Debaroti's face and somehow did not feel like disappointing. "Well, I don't know much about it either, I am a newcomer, too. But I've always found the cafeteria a favorable ground for relationships to develop. Students fall in and out of love here, at this very place. Long-term relationships begin. Not so happy endings for the unlucky ones, but a place of community and friendship."

She stopped in the middle of her conversation as her eyes fell upon an attractive young man who had just walked in.

Debaroti wasted no time. "Oh, I see you're interested in Arnab, the most popular guy in the campus. I grew up in the same neighborhood as him. I've basically known him since he was in diapers. I can introduce you to him if you want. But I will refrain myself from having anything to do with matters of heart. He is the college *Casanova* and has already broken many young hearts in his life. He has an irresistible liking for beautiful women and glides in and out in their company with his charming, smooth talk."

Arnab who seemed like he wasn't all too keen to order a coffee, stood scanning his surroundings, at once looking confused and expectant. His eyes caught Debaroti from a distance, but then noticed the timid girl who fell victim to Deborati's whimsical and overtly friendly behavior. He rested an elbow on one of the food counters and now, clasping his hands, pretended to look around aimlessly; every once in a while, checking to see if the new girl was still shooting glances in his direction.

In a short span of time, somehow, Deborati had forced her entire life story and freshman gossip all into one conversation. Tanusree, who had had enough, glanced at Arnab and casually smiled at him. Arnab immediately smiled back and began walking to their table uninvited.

"Hey Debi, you both seem to be sitting all by yourselves, do you mind if I join?" "And who is this, a new friend? May I have the pleasure of your name?" he began.

"Hi, I'm Tanusree. My friends call me Tanu," she replied bashfully.

"I just met her myself. She's a freshman enrolled in the physics department." Deborati then turned to Tanusree and said, "This is Arnab Chatterjee, a senior in Business College who had already made a name for himself by being involved with multifarious activities outside of campus.

"It's a pleasure," he said with a smile. "Chotku, bring three cups of hot coffee to our table, and make it real special." He beckoned a boy of about ten years old, the cafeteria's one and only waiter, as he passed by the table, precariously balancing three cups of tea in his hands.

Tanusree, who remained aloof about her family but lived in the same college city, was dropped off every day in an expensive chauffeur-driven car. One day, as she stepped out of the car, her steps although measured and poised, she stumbled onto the pavement with her books, which fell all around her. Arnab appeared from nowhere. He picked up her books helped her on her feet. An electrifying smile from Arnab was all that was needed to win her over.

As days rolled into months, the trio—Arnab, Tanusree and Debaroti—became inseparable. They sat at the same table every day after class and sipped hot coffee over long conversations, coupled with mirth and laughter. Soon Arnab showed his preference for Tanusree. His intense gaze at her, and jumping at every opportunity to please her, convinced Tanusree that their feelings were mutual, and that their friendship was progressing to another level. And so, began the countless number of dates, classes skipped, college rules broken. Even the thought of marriage had come up but they both decided to give it more time.

Deborati offered her friendly advice on the matter, "Wait until you finish your studies. Arnab too will finish in a year. And wouldn't it be proper for both of you to inform your parents and get their approval?" she asked.

"Of course, Debi, I'm aware of that," Tanusree replied.

Deborati asked, "Have you introduced him to your father or mother?"

Tanu's face paled at the mention of her family and she became quiet all of a sudden. Deborati could not help but think about the fact that Tanusree talked little about her personal life. She sometimes wondered about her friend's life outside the college. Tanusree never discussed having a father, a brother, or a sister. All she could guess from her friend's outward appearance was that she came from a well-to-do family here in the city.

One evening, Deborati and Arnab planned to surprise Tanusree by dropping in unannounced at her place. The maid answered the door and held it open with her foot, in her hands she carried a teapot.

"Who is here at my house unannounced?" asked a satin smoothed voice from the inner quarters of the house. A tall and willowy woman of considerable beauty made her appearance rather reluctantly to look at the guests.

"Some friends of Tanus, I believe." The maid turned around to answer.

The woman's eyes met the two young college students, her face contorted and turned white, and she disappeared to the inner room where she came from.

Debaroti thought that her rude behavior was a reflection of her awareness that she was an exquisite looking woman. The woman reappeared from the corner again, put her hand gently behind the maid's shoulder and quietly said, "Tanu has gone out with her uncle, but she should be home any minute. Malti, please serve them some tea outside here on the porch."

Arnab, who finally caught a look of the woman, retreated few steps backwards, as if he too had seen a ghost. "Oh Debi, I don't think it is a good idea sticking around here any longer. Let's go." He turned and began to climb down the stairs toward the street.

Debaroti, confused, forced an apologetic smile and hurried out after Arnab. Throughout the entire journey back, Arnab was quiet.

"What happened Arnab? It seemed like you knew her, did you? Am I right? Why did she make you feel so uncomfortable? Why did you behave like that?"

Sighing deeply, Arnab kept quiet and looked the other way. "Not today, Debi, some other time. Also, I think it's over between Tanu and I."

This made things worse for Debi as her mind now raced frantically amidst a universe of possibilities. Arnab didn't seem like he was in a mood to explain and neither did she deem it fair to push him. They had walked several blocks until Arnab stopped suddenly. He sat down on the curbside with his face covered in his hands, sobbing in tears.

"All right now, Arnab, calm down. It couldn't be that bad?"

"Yes, it could. She was one of the aberrant choices I made during my teenage years, a terrible mistake which will remain with me forever," He shook his head. "I flung myself into a life of pleasure, plunged headlong into an indulgence, as I rebelled against my parents in a mad, stupid craving for absolute freedom." He looked up at his friend. "It's hard to tell you what I'm going to tell you now," he continued.

"That woman, Tanu's mother, used to run a bordello here in this city where she entertained people from respectable backgrounds. During my high school days, I visited that place. I knew her ... I stopped going there eventually, but I..."

Arnab's voice was so quivery that Deborati had to grip his arm tightly even as she stood rooted to the spot, transfixed, not knowing what to say.

The next day Deborati found Tanusree after class and admitted to her about visiting her home yesterday and their abrupt departure.

Tanusree finally spoke out, "My mother told me that you bolted within minutes of meeting her. I'm sorry I haven't been forthcoming about my family. I lost my father when I was very young. He had an illness that dragged on for years depleting us emotionally and financially. After my father passed, his close friend Soumen, whom my mother told me to call Uncle Soumen, reached out to her with a letter of condolence. He showed up at my father's funeral and hovered around my mother all the time. My mother was overwhelmed at his kindness and generosity, but he began to make his presence felt by visiting us every evening and slowly entered our lives, taking advantage of our vulnerability."

Tanusree continued, "He was aware of my intense dislike for him, especially his presence in the house until late in the evenings. I thought he was trying to take my father's place, and I detested it. My mother wanted me to be nice to him and I would somehow manage to say few formal words to him. I told my mother to tell him that she did not want him around the house, and I somehow knew he was up to no good, but she could not bring herself to say anything to him. As years rolled on, she began to rely on him more and more. Uncle Soumen, who was also a wealthy businessman, was her security and she needed him to be around to provide for both of us. I hate to say it, but we needed him, and my mother would have sleepless nights at the thought of going hungry, begging in the streets. To my amazement, she slowly surrendered into his arms despite my vocal protestations."

"What happened then?" Deborati asked.

"As days went by, Uncle Souman admitted to owning a bordello here in the city. He started bringing the women who worked there into the house, who, eventually made it to the bedroom. My mother treated the first few visits with a feigned dismissal, but eventually, it got the better of her. Sometimes, at night I would hear her whimpering, tearfully begging him to spare her from that wretched confusion-filled existence. She was fearful for me as I was turning into an adolescent. Finally, one day I saw my mother on her knees. She pleaded with him promising him that if he left me alone, she would agree to work for him at the bordello. He agreed and kept his promise. As long as my mother works for him, I can continue to go to college."

Deborati sat dumbstruck, her eyes wide. She wanted to wrap Tanusree in her arms and hold her tightly, safe against the world, in a place of light and warmth.

"Oh, Tanu, I'm so sorry about everything. I don't know what to do. But I'm here for you and nothing will ever come between us, nobody is going to hurt you as long as

I'm here with you," said Deborati holding her arms open.

"But Debi, what I don't understand, is why you two ran away so abruptly after seeing my mother? How did you recognize her?" asked Tanusree confused.

It was Debaroti's turn to explicate Arnab's promiscuous background. Tanusree fell into Debaroti's lap in tears realizing that Arnab too was a client of her mother.

In the following months, Arnab completed his final year and never spoke to Tanusree or Deborati again. During the remainder of college, both girls remained the closest of friends, eating together at the cafeteria, walking to and from classes, and enjoying each other's company. The four years remained joyous to both. When it came time to graduate, Deborati received a job offer in Mumbai to follow her career in journalism. Tanusree remained in the city to live with her mother after college. The two lost touch over the years, until now, when they glanced at each other for the first time in twenty years at that college reunion.

Debaroti ran over to Tanusree with open arms and engulfed her body.

"It's so good to see you! You haven't changed one bit! What are you doing now? Where are you living? Are you married? Do you have children? Oh, remember that time in the cafeteria when we started dancing and we got kicked out? Have I told you how good it is to see you!"

Tanusree smiled back without saying anything, enjoying her friends energetic voice after all these years. Finally, after some time she replied back, "After college, I worked in the physics lab, but unfortunately, my mother fell ill after a few years and she passed away. I now work for Uncle Saumon," her smile lingered for a moment, but then dissipated.

Debaroti grabbed her again and hugged her tightly. The two women sat down together after all these years and continued to bond like once before. Debaroti, who promised Tanusree to be there for her from now on, immediately began planning for Tanusree to move to Mumbai with her. As the night ended, the ladies walked out the door together hand in hand, acknowledging *a little bit of yesterday*, but looking ahead to a more promising tomorrow.

LONESOME

ADITI STOOD AT the window of her bedroom holding a hot cup of tea in her hand just like every other evening. She took a sip from the cup and slowly put the cup back on the saucer, then rested it on the windowsill. Outside, the dusk descended, engulfing the sky in semi darkness, but only to be illuminated after a short while by the moonlight, accompanied by a star-studded sky. It was going to be a chilly night and strong gusty winds had already started to shake the leafless branches silhouetted against the sky. In the dark, the branches resembled skeletons swaying from the trees above. Street lamps lit up at the corners of sidewalks and shed light into the darkness as evening drew closer. Aditi shuddered as she looked out of the window and quickly wrapped herself with a shawl that she found on the bed.

A young married couple had just moved into a condominium across the street. Aditi developed a curiosity about them for no apparent reason. The window in her bedroom had venetian blinds. She rotated the blinds from the open position to closed by pulling the cords. Moving one of the slats to peak through, Aditi watched the newlyweds unobserved. She stationed herself at the same spot not knowing that their presence would soon have a profound effect on her own married life.

As the shades of evening drew nearer and nearer, she took a shower, put on some perfume, and dressed up as if she was going out to dinner. Aditi adorned herself in an expensive silk dress, powdered her face and tucked a red rose, neatly into her long graying hair. She dismissed her maid and waited anxiously for her husband to come home. She flung the door wide open as soon as she heard the doorbell.

"There you are! I was watching the road, waiting for you to come home. How was your day, my dear?" There was a coquettish tone in her voice as she threw herself upon him, hanging about his neck, almost strangling him with her bejeweled arms.

"Oh Akhil, wouldn't it be nice if we could go out to eat? I believe *Regal* makes the best *biryani*. I haven't had them for a long time," she implored.

Akhil, who was somber from a long day, was taken aback. He looked at his wife with puzzling eyes. He was not ready for the theatrical performance from someone to whom he had been married for the last thirty-four years. He abruptly freed himself from her embrace, slipped into a chair to watch the evening news.

"Not today, Aditi, I'm dead tired with so much pressure at work, I want to take it easy at home."

Her desire to go out and eat dinner with her husband was blown away in a matter of seconds by her husband's reluctance and apathy. The soft glow that was radiating from her face lost its luminance as tears streamed down her cheeks. She slowly undid her hair and let it fall to its full length in exasperation.

"Look Akhil, please don't treat me this way, I'm your wife. You didn't even ask me how I was when you came in, didn't pay any attention to what I wore. I spent two hours in front of the mirror just to dress up for you! I wore the dress that you gave me on my birthday three years back, how can you not remember?"

She sobbed, stomped angrily towards the kitchen to warm up the evening dinner. In her dismay, she realized with bitterness that Akhil had built up an invisible wall over the years, detached from his wife. The spark that once kindled their love had been extinguished without ever a clear defining moment. The evenings when he came home from work were not the same as they used to be, the arms that used to hold her tight lay limp on his sides.

Akhil got up from the dinner table after finishing his food. "The lentil soup was too salty today," he remarked.

She paid little heed to these criticizing remarks. They had become inconsequential over the years. After dinner, whilst he listened to the news, she sat on a separate couch reading a book. She never had interest in the things happening around the world. It was hard for her to constantly hear news of internecine feuds in troubling parts of the world. "What do I care for Syrian refugees or Putin's Ukraine strategy. Why can't we simply watch a movie together?" she thought.

Before bed time, Aditi prepared tea for Akhil and took her cup of tea and entered her bedroom. She slowly rotated the blinds, this time from closed position to an open position, and peeked through them.

"Isn't that wonderful, a perfect picture of love and romance", she thought about the young lad with a bunch of flowers in his hand, kissing his beloved wife.

It brought a surge of memories of the days when Akhil

would stop by the florist on the way home every now and then to pick up some flowers for her. She loved colorful bouquets of mixed dahlias. She would cut the stem diagonally, add flower food into the water in the vase then insert the bouquet in the water. Some days, he surprised her with a bunch of red roses in their long thin stems.

"I saw these beautiful roses on my way home and I remembered how you loved the lovely fragrance of red roses," he would say.

One evening, while Aditi stood at the window of her bedroom with her usual cup of tea, Akhil came in.

"What's the matter with you Aditi, why are you acting so strange nowadays? You're always staring through these blinds," he looked at her puzzled.

Taken unawares, she withdrew herself from the window, but then on second thought, she took a hold of her husband's hand and pointed towards the young couple living across the street.

"I watch them every evening. Look how adorable they are, I've never seen a young couple like them, so loving and devoted to each other. Look how he laid out vegetables on the kitchen counter. He is probably going to cook today," she said and smiled at her husband.

Aditi remembered the days when the children were young. She used to get up before everyone else, cooked everything ahead of time on the weekend, that way she did not have to cook for the rest of the week. She used the dishes that were frozen which made cooking not an issue at all. Now she was close to sixty and was still in the work force. She loved the idea of retirement, only to realize that with her children gone she would be awfully *lonesome* in the house. Twice a week she picked up groceries from the market, sometimes her grocery bags would overflow with multiple items of basic necessities. Akhil would never stir or lift a finger.

When she invited people for dinner, she was the one who planned the menu, ran to several stores to tick mark the shopping list, and cooked nine courses of dinner. After that, she would have to clean the house and arrange the flowers. The aftermath of the parties was what she abhorred when her husband made halfhearted offers to help her. There were times when she thought that Akhil should be so fortunate to have her – a wife that cooks, cleans, and takes care of everything – and that if she ever left, he likely would not even be capable of turning on the stove.

The next day Aditi bought a bouquet of fresh flowers and handed it to her husband. "How about you start trimming the stems and place the flowers in water. Use the glass vase that is on the shelf. And those two heavy grocery bags in the car needed to be brought inside," she continued.

"I am watching a college football game, can it wait?" He retorted.

"The milk has been sitting in the car for a while, plus there are lot of other things that may lose their freshness."

Akhil cursed under his breath, but he got up, slammed the door, and brought in the groceries.

"Thanks, dear," she smiled and took his hands in hers. "I only wanted to do things together, I'm tired of doing things all on my own."

"You have some mental problems," he blurted out. "I could make an appointment for you with a psychiatrist if you want. By the way, where did you get those ideas of doing things together? We did a lot of that stuff together when we were young, but you should try to accept the things as they are now. Accept the life that we built together, Aditi. Things have changed, you have to let go your past, and we are not young anymore."

He resumed watching the football game and after the game was over, he picked up the thread of the conversation.

"Why don't you go out and make new friends, join a coffee or book club. Go to the gym, explore and be on your own. The only way to be happy is to carve out a life for you; try to be self-reliant instead of depending on me."

"I want to be just the two of us, the way we were, remember how we used to go to the parks every evening, strolling by holding hands together, munching on freshly roasted peanuts, buying fritters from wayside vendors? Oh, how I miss those days, Akhil! We can still have them if we want them."

"Don't you think it is quite fulfilling that we are still married and living under the same roof? What more of a happier situation did you expect?"

She ran into her room and stood near the window, but she did not see the young man and his wife, the next day also she waited for them eagerly and made enquiries regarding their whereabouts. One neighbor said they heard a terrible fight a couple of days back, and she packed her suitcase and left him. Aditi felt disheartened at the news, after all they were like her own children, and she yearned to know what went wrong?

Aditi eventually enrolled her name in a ladies club and started gym classes. She made new friends within a short span of time and spent more hours at the movie theatres. At home, she listened to her old favorite songs, completely relaxed.

Six months later, Aditi realized that her thirty-fifth anniversary of her wedding was in sight. However, the anniversary came around and she asked her husband how he would like to celebrate their wedding anniversary, he said, "I can't, my dear. I must go to work. Things are getting worse, and I am overwhelmed with the stress at the job."

"But tonight is our special night," she protested. "I shall dismiss the cook for the evening, and I'll cook the dinner. It will be just us two alone together on our wedding day." She smiled at him.

She planned a romantic dinner at home. She thoughtfully prepared a menu, baked salmon with rice and brussels sprouts. She took out the nice set of crystal glasses that he bought for her. She laid the table with fancy plates and silverware. In the center of the table, she put a vase with elegant roses, and lit several candles before he came into the house. The stereo played a soft, slow music that they both enjoyed.

Akhil did not fail to notice this sudden turn of her resentment and her lifestyle. He felt amused at the outcome of his small advice.

"She may not have to see a psychiatrist after all", he humored himself.

One morning, she left her cup of tea on the table to follow her husband to the front door, planted a kiss on his cheek, closed the door and went back to her cooling tea that was heated up twice already. That evening of the same day, when he came home, he found a note neatly tucked under the antique vase that they had had for a long time, a wedding gift. She had put some forget-me-not flowers, slightly wilted now, into the vase. He saw the note under the vase, picked it up, and read it:

I wanted to make us happy, but I failed in my attempts to do so. For now, I am alone. And this constant fear of being alone has driven me to my decision. You did not want to be with me, and our marriage has stagnated over the years. I believed things would change for the better; unfortunately, things will never change. No matter what is happening to our marriage, I still have to go on with my life. I would have given anything to be loved and respected. I have decided to walk away from you. Wish you all the best.

Akhil sat down on the kitchen table, lost in a deep thought. After some time, he got up to prepare food for himself for the first time in years, however, fumbled to turn the stove on.

HISTORICAL RECONCILIATION

"WATCH YOUR STEP. I have a surprise for you at the top! Be careful, some of these steps are pretty steep."

Chandra guided her teacher as she cautiously stepped on the uneven cracks and voids over large areas of the steps. Exposure to weather and centuries of traffic took its toll on the entrance to the Acropolis of Athens. On both sides of the steps, limestone rocks of different sizes and shapes were strewn all over. Chandra waited until she was on the last step that led to one the most revered temples from the *Classical Greek* period, the Parthenon. A shadow of its former glory, the remaining structure still stood on delicate marble columns, drawing thousands of visitors from every corner of the world.

Anjana Das, nodded at Chandra, reassuringly. "Of course, I am trying to be as careful as I can," she retorted, as she placed another foot forward, bending down to catch her breath.

"Just this way, we have to follow this path up to the top. I have something to show you!"

Both of them were fascinated by the legends of Greek history. The *Classical period* when Greece reached its zenith of power and glory, both politically and culturally and was a favorite topic of conversation between the two history enthusiasts. Chandra had even previously published scholarly work on Greek tragedies with historical emphasis of the author and poet Homer, that was peer-reviewed internationally.

Chandra still recalled the first day she met her history professor. With a mind that was fully enriched with historical stories of the *Trojan Wars*, the disarmingly beautiful face of Helen of Troy – *the face that launched a thousand ships* – Chandra had imagined her history professor to be a similarly enchanting and captivating mentor. Instead, Professor Anjana Das, who entered the classroom looked far different from the legendary Greek queen. She was quite an unattractive woman of ambiguous age. Her hair was combed up and twisted together at the back of her head, endowing her with a stumpy appearance. Underneath those oblique eyes, she had a large flat nose, and her bushy eyebrows sprawled above the square black frame of her eyeglasses like untamed wildflowers. When she smiled, which she rarely did, a row of *paan* stained teeth protruded contrasting her worn out face. But ugly as she was, there was something forgiving about her nature. A feeling of sadness came over her as Chandra, who decided to sit up close in the second row, being that is was difficult to hear her. She quickly realized why the remainder of the class avoided the first two rows, when she was provided with a generous salivary spray that came with the professors' rhapsodic lectures.

Professor Anjana Das was one of four faculty members of the history department. She stood out amongst her colleagues by being uncouth, unsophisticated, and strange in her mannerisms. And yet, she was an excellent teacher; she was passionate about her subject, and her teaching style kept her students spellbound. They were lucid and vivid, making her lectures entertaining by garish anecdotes. She was confident and expected her students to attend her classes with complete undivided attention.

Chandra felt a strong connection to her professor. During her first semester, she received the highest grade in the class. The following day, Anjana called Chandra in to her office.

"Chandra, you have lots of potential, I noticed you have quite depth of knowledge of history and you share a similar passion to interpret the meaning behind historical sciences. You would do very well in a career in history." She threw in some encouraging words for her which brought tears into Chandra's eyes.

Anjana would let Chandra borrow books from her from time to time for additional reading. On the pretext of returning a book that she borrowed from her, Chandra one day went to her house after school.

Anjana opened the door and greeted her. The house was considerably big for a single person but modest and free from unnecessary extravaganza. There was a dark wood coffee table with two drawers in the center of the living room, a dark brown color leather sofa, quite contemporary in an old house. Patterned cushions of beige color stood out against the sofas. There were two glass corner tables that did not match with anything. The remainder of the walls and shelves were filled with old trinkets and souvenirs from the countless trips and different parts of the world she had visited.

"Do you enjoy living all alone?" Chandra asked.

"Not always, there are days when I get lonely, but over the years I have gotten used to it. I came into possession of this house after parents died," she said. "Maybe you would like to have a tour of the house after we have tea. There are rooms in this house that I hardly use, only seldom when my nieces and nephews visit me."

"Oh, that's nice. I'm sure they are fond of you," Chandra said.

"I am the oldest in my family. My father had a mental illness and for that matter he could not hold on to a job very long. His career was interrupted again and again by his illness, and finally he had to give up teaching school. Slowly, a severe depression got hold of him. It was only a matter of time before he took to bed with the incurable disease. As for my younger sister and brother, it was I who had to take care of them once my father passed away."

Chandra decided to dig deeper into her professor's life to learn more about her. "Were you ever married or in love?" she asked.

Anjana paused and looked down at her fingers. After a while she continued with her story in small fragments.

"I was never married, but I was in love. He belonged to a very well to do *Brahmin* family. Unfortunately, I came from a middle class *Kayastha* family." Anjana, in one of the few times Chandra had ever seen, smiled. "He was the love of my life, the one and only. I was already a teacher at that time. He was in medical school. The question of a union between the two of us was unthinkable and preposterous for both families. His parents arranged a marriage for him with a girl from the same caste. My mother had her own reasons for not wanting her daughter to be married. Who would look after the family once I left?"

Chandra questioned further, "So did you ever see him again?"

"Unfortunately, yes, he and I continued to see each other after his betrothal, in secret rendezvous. But we knew we could never have one another; our love was destined to fall apart. It all ended when I found myself with an unplanned pregnancy with him. Sadly, he did not want to tell his parents because of how they might react."

Anjana stopped in the middle of her narration and offered to bring in some refreshments.

"But what about your own family, didn't they give you some sort of support?" Chandra asked.

"Being unmarried and pregnant, I was asked to quit my job. My mother did not take the news favorably. She refused to be a part of the condition I was in. The stigma of premarital pregnancy ruined my future marriage prospects." She shifted in her chair and faced Chandra directly. "But I decided to have the baby and it was a beautiful baby girl. When I told him about his new daughter, he struggled tremendously on whether to leave and raise the child with me. Ultimately, he decided to stay and not disappoint his parents. And sadly, in a mixed state of mind, I gave my child up for adoption and ran away from home. There isn't a day that I don't think about her and I regretted that decision." She sighed, as years had now exhausted her tears. "Now, let's have tea and we can talk about the Roman Empire and the *Baths of Caracalla.*"

Her teacher's life story brought tears to Chandra's eyes, and on her way back home she promised herself that someday she would do something kind for her teacher. Over the next few months, the teacher and student bonded over many afternoons over tea and conversations about Greek philosophers and famous battles that took place between ruling empires. The school year was nearing to an end, when Chandra decided to surprise Anjana with a trip to Greece, one of their favorite places to discuss its history. On the very last day of class, Chandra stayed behind the classroom and surprised her with tickets to go visit together.

"This is so incredibly kind of you, Chandra. No one has ever given me such a gift. You are truly a gift from God. I would love to go on a trip with you, but I don't think my frail body can handle the traveling anymore."

After much persistence, Chandra pleaded with Anjana to make the trip with her and ultimately, she gave in. The two prepared to spend a full week together exploring different parts of Greece. They saved the last day to go visit the Parthanon where Chandra had planned to give her one more gift.

The two climbed to the top of amongst the difficult steep steps that led to the century old temple grounds. High above the city peering down, Chandra and Anjana stood there in astonishment at the beauty that surrounded them. Anjana in between her breaths spoke, "This is incredible. I can't believe we did it. All the way up here. Never did I think I would get to see this."

She began to start crying. This was the first time Chandra had seen her worn face develop tears again. Chandra smiled, "I have one more gift to give you."

She opened up her backpack up and took out an envelope and handed it to her.

"What is this, my dear?" asked Anjana. She opened the envelope and found an old document, a hospital discharge certificate with the name, "Chandra Das." The dates matched the same time when Anjana had given up her child for adoption. At first, Anjana could not utter a word, as her fingers began to tremble. She looked up to see Chandra, who smiled back in tears.

"It's me, mother." She gave in to a gush of tears that began to roll down her face. "When I turned eighteen years old, I went back to my orphanage and asked for my birth certificate, and I've been searching for you ever since," she explained. "When I found out you were a history teacher, I knew I had to find a way to get back to you. How I wished that I could tell you sooner, but I thought we could spend this trip together and enjoy this *historical reconciliation.*"

Anjana, still trembling and now in tears, opened her arms and held Chandra tightly. The mother and daughter did not let go for quite some time, enjoying the beautiful history around them and the history they shared together.

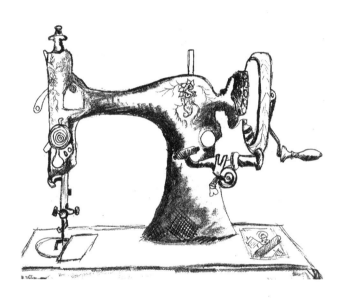

A DANGEROUS MIND

KABIR WAS A *DARZI*, a tailor by trade who carried on a family tailoring business. Like his two older brothers, he began working for his father at the age of twelve. But unlike his brothers, his pattern making skills was appreciated amongst his customers.

In the morning, he opened his shop by untangling the weathered chains and vintage locks that secured the shutters. At the door to the shop, a shabby square signboard dangled in the wind, hanging precariously on a rusty nail, with *Kabir's Tailoring Shop* written in clear, bold letters. It was the only piece of identification of his meager business. The shop was a small room equipped with two chipped, antique Singer sewing machines, the whirring sound of which made it necessary for everyone to talk loudly. A noisy oscillating fan brought relief from the scorching summer, and faint music from a small radio created a diversion to the monotony of his tedious work.

A clutter of fabrics cut in different shapes, reels of thread, and laces and beads were heaped in boxes that lined the walls. In a small open box in a corner, a faded measuring tape, bobby pins, and sewing needles were stacked. The floor itself was strewn with tiny colorful threads, one or two pair of heavy scissors, marking chalks, pencils, tracing wheel and paper. And at the far end of the room, stood an iron.

Stripped down to the waist and wearing nothing but a blue and yellow checkered *lungi*, Kabir sat crossed legged on the floor measuring and cutting fabric. Sometimes, his eyes narrowed as he looked through his thick glasses to place a thread spool on the spool pin of the sewing machine. When a customer came in, he would rub the texture of a fabric with the tip of his fingers, by which he could tell the quality of the material. Next, he would use his measuring tape to take the customer's exact measurements, note them on the cloth with a lead pencil and then using sharp scissors to cut the fabric with perfect precision.

The sewing room was adjacent to his thatched roof house where he lived with his wife and daughter. Both mother and daughter were engaged in works of lesser skills, diligently sewing the seams, and buttons into garments. They were excellent at making alterations, repairing holes or worn areas in fabric using needle and thread alone. They could fix any tear, rip, missing button, loose hem, or poor fit and they made the repair work as invisible and neat as possible.

One afternoon, while Kabir was busy with his usual work of cutting and measuring, he looked up to see Gofur Minja at the door. He hurriedly ushered him into his shop with a hearty welcome. Being a man of importance, Gofur was rare sight in the village. He seldom visited anybody in person unless it was a matter of consequence. He was also a *darzi* by trade but owned several acres of land and was well known in the village as a wealthy landlord. The villagers respected him and wanted to be in his good books.

"How's your business going Kabir?" Gofur asked.

"We are getting along, by the grace of God, the business is slow during off season but picks up again during festival time. We could always do a little better with a bit of extra money; we are sometimes working hand to mouth." Kabir went on breathlessly, he was too overwhelmed by the wealthy darzi and the very fact he was standing in his own humble shop. "By next rainy season I need to replace my roof, the rainwater seeps through the broken tiles. Every time it rains, I put a bucket underneath the hole to collect water."

"I see," Gofur said. "Try to get more orders, that way you can make more money."

Gofur went on to advise Kabir how to expand his business. But suddenly he changed the topic of his conversation into a more relevant one, and the true reason for his visit.

"How's Nazma doing? I had a glimpse of her the other day as I was passing by. She has grown up and turned into a remarkably good-looking girl. I'm thinking of bringing her into my family as my older son is ready to be married. We are looking for a girl just like her."

"Of course, I'm pleased that you're thinking about her, and I'm sure your son will be a perfect match for my daughter. Her mother also keeps reminding me to find a suitable groom for her. But before I say anything, I want to ask Nazma. She is an intelligent girl and does well in school. She wants to learn more," Kabir replied.

"But you have no means to send her to college. I think she is better off staying home and being a wife to my son." Gofur retorted.

"Please give me some time to think it over and talk with my wife. I'll let you know." Kabir answered politely.

Kabir had only one dream and that was for his daughter to be more than a seamstress. As he measured and cut fabric all afternoon, he thought of what Gofur had said. "I will never allow Nazma to follow the footsteps of her father and grandfather," he said to himself. "The life of a seamstress is the last thing I will ever bestow upon my child. She has to pursue her education and be a professional, a teacher, a lawyer if she wants to be. But what about my brothers and my uncles and all the others who disagree?" He thought with a frown. "They will throw me out of their community if I tell them about my plan to send Nazma to school! And now that Gofur has asked for Nazma's hand in marriage for his son. How can I refuse him? What can I do?"

The chances for a better education for Nazma were minimal. The cost of sending her to college was beyond his means and the long distances she had to cover to reach even the nearest one needed to be reckoned with.

"We could all move to the city, Nazma had suggested several times. "Rahim uncle asked us many times to go and live there, and a bigger place means more customers for you."

"No, my dear child," he had always replied. "I have thought about it a lot of times, but I belong to this community, this village, and my ancestral home. How can I leave everybody when we are all kith and kin?"

After a month or so, Rahim came to the village to place orders. He was a close friend of Kabir and owned a tailor shop in a big city that was thriving quite well. Whenever he had large numbers of sewing orders, he brought some to Kabir to help his business out as well.

"What do you think of my suggestion to come live in the city?" Rahim suddenly asked Kabir.

"I never seriously considered it, but Nazma has brought it up," Kabir answered. "I think she wants to go to the city since she dreams about going to a good college."

"Since she is good in her studies, I don't see why she shouldn't come, even if you won't. Nazma can work part time in my tailoring shop, finish high school, and help to pay for her tuition."

At Rahim's insistence, Kabir and his wife decided to send Nazma to the city. But Nazma's pursuit of higher education had an adverse effect in the village amongst the other *darjis*. They thought it was a breach of faith. A girl's place was at home, helping with the household chores and taking care of the family. Gofur was enraged beyond measure. He took it as a personal insult when Kabir's daughter refused to marry his son, especially since he was such an important person in the village and Kabir had no status or money.

The entire *darji* community showed their disapproval by shunning Kabir and his family in every way. Kabir and his wife were excluded from all the social gatherings, and sometimes their friends even ignored their presence when encountered in the marketplace. Kabir and his wife became the target of ridicule, harassment. and were subjected to a passive aggression all because they wanted their daughter to have the opportunity to be educated.

One morning, Kabir's wife went to the one and only communal well of the village to fill up a bucket of water. The entire village depended on that tube-well water. Women and children usually queued up with buckets. It was also a place for idle talks amongst the village women, and on this day, all the gossip was about Nazma.

When asked why she returned home with an empty bucket, Kabir's wife replied, "Everyone at the well was gossiping about Nazma. Gofur's wife was the loudest of them all. Not only that, one of them removed my bucket from the queue. I couldn't stand to stay there any longer." With tears in her eyes, she threw the bucket into the yard so hard it made a dent.

Kabir sat on the threshold of his house and covered his face. He was in agony. The social ostracism went a step further when one morning Kabir saw graffiti on his door written with colorful chalk. The sense of loss of place in the village and the craving for a sense of belonging to a community drove him into depression. His self-esteem and a meaningful existence came to nothingness. Furthermore, it dealt a heavy blow to his pride, when Gofur decided to marry his son to Nazir Bhai's daughter Saira instead of Nazma.

Worn down with harassment and anger from the disparaging behavior of the villagers, Kabir's heart became fixated with the dream of a better life. He was a strong-willed person, and his sky-reaching ambitions for his daughter helped him to look forward to an idealistic future. He learned to distance himself from his tormentors and started to believe in a world far beyond his rural, ramshackle ancestral home.

He wrote to Rahim saying that he had decided to go to the city and work at his shop, and Rahim wrote back that he was welcome to come and was happy at the thought that Nazma would be glad to have her parents in the city as well.

"Don't you think you made a good choice, the right decision to come to the city?" Rahim remarked, who had always stood by his side, always eager to help him.

"I will still miss my village, but for the time being, it is a novel idea to move to the city. I am blessed that Nazma can go to college and get a degree," Kabir answered.

A year passed by, and with Rahim's help, Kabir was able to open a tailor shop of his own in the city. Kabir seemed to be seeing better days. His business was picking up and he saved all his money to send his daughter to college.

As it turned out, Nazma proved herself to be highly motivated in her studies and got distinctions in three subjects. She enrolled in a women's college and did so well that she scored highest in her class. But Nazma's mother still had old fashion plans for her daughter.

"Once she graduates, it will be appropriate for her to get married to an equally educated groom." Her mother said one evening.

"There is no rush to get her married so soon," Kabir replied. "She could still go for further studies."

When Kabir told Rahim that Nazma's mother was hoping for a wedding soon, Rahim said, "How about sending Nazma to America? She would be the first girl from this generation of *darjis* to study abroad."

"It is always in my mind that Nazma would get a degree from a foreign country." Kabir answered, his eyes brightened at the prospect. "But how can I finance her studies?"

It so happened that Rahim's brother, Khalid, lived in New York and owned a restaurant in the financial district of Manhattan. "I could ask my brother to get some information on that matter," Rahim replied. "She could apply for scholarships and financial assistance."

And so, started the long process of filling out application forms to enroll in a college, in a different country, and a totally different environment. Nazma, too, began to dream passionately about going to America. She watched American television commercials and flipped through the pages of periodicals and magazines that featured news about America. Kabir was not surprised to find books by American authors underneath her pillow. They fanned her hopes and aspirations, a belief in the possibility of educational opportunities, and she dreamed of a bright future.

Eventually all the paperwork was done, and the answers came back: Nazma was accepted to a university with good scholarships. So, when she had the first glimpse of The Statue of Liberty, coming to New York, Nazma could not help but think about *Emma Lazarus* and her poem, *The New Colossus*, offering a warm welcome to all immigrants. "*A mighty woman with a torch, from her beacon-hand, glows world-wide welcome.*"

New York fascinated her. She walked most of the time, although some days she used the subway and the bus system when they were the fastest way to her destination. Sometimes she took a walk on an elevated path of the High Line to view the Manhattan Skyline as well as the other buildings. Nazma stopped at Time Square to stare at the well-lit buildings and billboards, and people walking in the streets of New York at any given time of the day or night delighted her. She started relishing the roadside food and music played by amateurs on the sidewalks. All at once, her attention was drawn towards the iconic twin towers of the World Trade Center, the hub of the bustling financial district. They were both monumentally tall and a major tourist attraction. All these days she had only seen the pictures, and now she was thrilled at the thought that she was experiencing it to the full. How fortunate was to be right here at this moment when everybody in her village had no idea what she was perceiving.

Soon she began to see herself as a New Yorker, trying to keep up with her intensive business classes and holding a part time job at Khalid's restaurant in the financial district. Some days, her studies and her work as a waitress turned out to be overwhelming. She hated when Khalid was impatient with her skills as a waitress.

One morning, she spilled coffee on a customer who happened to be quite a decent looking young man in his late twenties. He frequented the eatery on a regular basis.

"Bear with me on this one she said, ugh what a mess! I guess I'll go and grab the paper towel roll to clean this up," said Nazma, shaken up.

"It's okay, it's a matter of no importance to me. Don't worry about it. It's only coffee. By the way, I am Fayez," he smiled at her, disregarding the stain the spilled coffee left on his white shirt.

Taken by surprise, Nazma turned to look at him and caught him gazing deep into her eyes. What she saw in his eyes she did not want to look away from, for, in those brilliant brown eyes, she saw a promise, a promise so sincere, so unwavering, that she couldn't look away. And thus, began their friendship which turned into courtship and marriage. Back at home, Nazma's and Fayez's marriage was a time for celebration. Kabir and his wife could not expect a better husband for their daughter. They did not have to worry about dowry or wedding expenses. He distributed sweets amongst his friends and relatives saying it was a great blessing that Nazma found a suitable husband.

Four years went by, Nazma graduated and started working for a small company and Fayez, too, was working hard. They were initially quite happy in their marriage, but Nazma began to notice that her husband would come home at late hours. He spent more time at the restaurant with Khalid. Disquieting thoughts and anxieties crept into her heart.

"You came home very late last night," she said one morning. "I waited for you."

"I was with Khalid," he said abruptly. He paused and then continued, "We were discussing a new business venture. It was gracious of him to offer me a chance to become his partner."

"But both of us are doing good jobs, why do you even think of starting a business now when we do not have any reserved money?"

"Let's not talk about it now," he said. "I need to get some sleep."

After that night, the topic of starting a business did not surface again. But there were some discernible changes in her husband's way of life that Nazma did not fail to notice. Her fun-loving husband became reclusive. He started bringing stacks of paper and books and became immersed in them. He would keep a black journal with him at all times and wrote down notes regularly. His religious practices became more regular and intensive. He did not miss his prayer time. Fayez started to believe in an idealism that was far beyond her comprehension. At dinner table, a very few words were exchanged, most of the time it was some insignificant words that were spoken between the two them. They began to see each other very little. After he came back from work, he read, prayed, and wrote in his journal. A feeling of anxiety and apprehension stirred inside her, and she became more and more troubled with a foreboding sense of something unusual.

It was in the midst of the ups and downs of their relationship that Nazma gave him the good news that he was going to be a father soon. Fayez was at first overjoyed and the thought of having a child brought about a noticeable change in him. It was a turn around to his former self, and soon he began to pay attention to his wife's needs with a renewed love and affection. The prospect of having a baby had a positive impact on their waning relationship and hope for a new beginning.

Then one evening, Fayez came home quite late with carrying a new briefcase.

"What do you have in that case?" Nazma asked.

Fayez paused and then said, "They are my usual stuff, my office papers."

Nazma decided not to ask her husband anything more for fear of reprisals. But the roots of suspicion began to grow inside her once more. Her baby was getting bigger and was expected to be delivered sometime in the second week of September.

Fayez took Nazma out for a walk one night and found themselves in the lower part of Manhattan. Fayez looked up at the buildings and said, "Nazma, I will be out of town for a few days. I have some business to take care of. It will be a good idea for you to stay home while I'm away. The briefcase I brought home the other day has money for you in case of emergency. It's there for you to use."

Nazma thought she heard a quiver in his voice.

"Where will you be? What if I have my contractions at that time? What will I do? You are not even a little bit concerned? Fayez, it's your baby, too, remember!" She started yelling at him in tears. "You don't have any compassion for me, how I wished I had gone to my parent's house for my confinement. I don't want to go through this alone. You should be with me." Nazma's eyes welled up, but she wiped them off silently.

The morning of September 11th, Nazma jolted out of her sleep by an unprecedented noise as her whole building shook. She ran out of her room to look out the living room window, and what she saw complete chaos. In the horizon above her, what once stood the massive Twin Towers, now were engulfed with black smoke. Hundreds of people on the street were running away from the destruction. Amidst the streaking ambulance lights and alarms, she ran to her television and learned that the unthinkable had happened as the two towers of World Trade Center were struck by airplanes, killing thousands of people. When the towers collapsed, a pall of choking smoke billowed through the streets. She could not grasp the enormity of the situation. She tried to call her husband again and again, but his phone was not picking up. In an instant, pain came rushing down her lower abdomen and she felt the harsh contractions. Within minutes, her water broke, and she laid down on the floor. She called for emergency but in light of the devastation occurring outside, emergency response took nearly an hour before arriving. That evening, alone without Fayez by her side, she delivered a baby girl.

For Nazma, her world fell apart as the whole story about the attack came to her knowledge. She agonized for Fayez and Khalid, who were both discovered to be radicalized individuals by al-Qaeda fundamentalists, and the co-conspirators in the heinous acts. Nazma had given the black journal to the authorities anonymously, which gave detailed information about the attack and of the nineteen other individuals who were al-Queda terrorists involved. Stricken to the core of her heart and now the increased persecution of Muslims in America, she quickly wanted to go back home with her new infant.

At first, Nazma was overwhelmed by the loss and abandonment. "It's all gone now, it's history," she thought. She found herself in direct confrontation with an uncertain future, perhaps a vague promise of an ideal life that was not realized. Fayez at times made her feel frustrated, but she felt protected and loved when he was there. She tried to remember her husband with kind memories, the good time they spent together. But then again, she would become engulfed by a rush of emotions, perpetuated by his crimes and the thought of harboring such *a dangerous mind*. At last, at the very moment of fear and desolation, she took solace in the birth of her daughter on that same fateful day. The birth of her daughter symbolized hope and opening up of a new chapter in her life. She looked at her daughter and realized that this was her baby, her beautiful miracle, pure happiness. She gazed lovingly at her newborn, and in that instant her whole life changed forever. Holding her, hearing her voice, Nazma knew right then nothing would ever be the same.

ON THE BANKS OF RIVER SARAYU

THE RIVER SARAYU flowed on endlessly. Forever meandering along small villages sitting on her banks, she grew wider every year with silt and age, building wisdom along her way about the impermanence of all things that surrounded her.

She played her part mutely. At times, she observed villagers submerge their young at her banks, some of who seemed rejuvenated and reborn once they were brought out of the water. At other times, a child, wrapped in white, offered to be engulfed in a raging pyre near her banks. The moon and stars shed silverlight upon it, and when the fire died out, the memory of the child was consecrated to her, the ashes strewn across her surface with flower petals, sent floating and tilting to the other side. Oddly, it felt similar to when the infants were bathed near her shallows, but still, it was different. Sad faces would then linger at her banks looking for comfort. She obliged, softly hugging the shores with her waves, with the moon's consent.

While rejoicing at the newness of life on earth and its joyful creatures, Sarayu bereaved with them at their sudden departures from their mortal bodies. She embraced the tears of their grief-stricken hearts into her warm waters as she flowed on, leaving no trace of the sorrowful moments. The winds in the distant skies asked her, *why would you lament at the unforeseen fate of the people? It is the order of the universe, although the time of dissolution was far distant, it had surely to come someday, so why lament now?*

How did Sarayu befriend them? It was the *ghat*, the broad flight of concrete steps that led down to the river where the villagers went to take a dip in the water and for their ablutions.

The ancient banyan tree near the banks of the river was where the villagers usually gathered. It was much like a town square where the peasants gathered. Some lingered smoking hookahs, while others exchanged quick hellos and left. The tree, like the river, symbolized eternity, antitheses of life that the villagers respected and held sacred. The banyan tree covered a considerable piece of land with its prop roots, providing for comfortable congregation. There stood a small deity under the tree where the village women lit a *diya* every evening.

He arrived at the bank before sunrise. Bending over, he touched his toes and then stretching out with his hands folded over his head, he said *Om*. After repeating this motion several times, he took deep breaths and then started walking towards the river. Knee deep into the water, he faced eastward and folded his hands in performance of *Surya Pranam,* a worship of the sun. In time, with the skies turning crimson and crows taking their first flight, he emerged from the water.

About a lifetime ago, he had decided to sever all ties with the material world and seek solitude, seek the Almighty in the mountains. With time his head had become home to a mass of matted dreadlocks, black and gray and his singular attire of a saffron robe had become ragged and soiled. His face, which still retained its old handsomeness was beginning to wrinkle and a thick scraggly beard descended down towards his chest. He sat under the banyan tree, cross-legged in a yoga posture and immersed himself in deep meditation.

Daybreak brought with it the first bathers and soon the banks of Sarayu were populated with village folk. They pushed and shoved trying to get a view, a few lurked around the Sadhu wondering where he had come from, nobody had seen him in those parts before. Some took a few steps closer to have a better look at this strange ascetic, who, despite the gradually growing attention, had his eyes shut and was seemingly lost in prayer.

"Baba, where are you from?" Asked a man, having picked up the courage to approach him one day and start a conversation. He opened his eyes and regarded the man standing before him, a village simpleton.

"I am from *Benares*, son." Looking at the small crowd that had gathered in front of the tree, he said, "I hope I am not inconveniencing your daily lives by occupying this spot. I was passing by and decided to stop here for a day or two to rest and meditate, it's getting hotter every day."

Voicing what seemed to be in everybody's mind, the man before him folded his hands and said, "Of course baba, you can stay here for as long as you want. We were simply curious to find someone like you in our corner of the village, we don't see too many sadhus passing by. Having you around will be a good thing for us."

The old man smiled and raised his hand in a sign of blessing and said, "I am grateful for your hospitality, I wouldn't come in the way of your daily tasks, you may ignore me, and have my thanks."

The villagers, having heard what he had to say, began dispersing one by one. Only a few children lingered, chewing on their nails and tentatively staring at the hairy stranger who again shut his eyes and, they thought, went back to sleep.

The next day, a few of the bathers heard the sadhu chanting the *Gayatri mantra*. Some stood at a distance listening while others squatted before him, admiring the stentorian quality of his voice. Often, at length, he would open his eyes to find a small crowd gathered before him, gaping and gawking as if at a rare bird. One afternoon, he found a plate of food kept neatly before him. It was covered with a piece of white cloth and next to it stood a glass of water. One of the wives must have come and dropped it off while he was lost in meditation. The food, twice a day, became a regularity, being provided by different families in turn.

One day, when a crowd had assembled before him under the banyan tree, he opened his eyes and spoke. "Dear all, I owe you my life, you have given me shelter and nourishment and with the grace of the Almighty I have been able to sit under the shade of this great tree and meditate. I have informed the Lord of your generosity and He has commanded me to reward you."

He reached into his cloth bag and pulled out a scroll of paper and proceeded to roll it out before him. The faces before him lit up. It was an astronomical chart with a large circle drawn in its center and various signs and etchings all around it. The chart depicted the positions of planets and stars, designed to give a skilled reader clues about what people's futures beheld. The villagers, being quite worried about the fate of their crops and their daughters, had always had a yearning to know what the stars augured and immediately a hushed whisper broke out among the people.

An old man came forth and said, "Baba, my daughter was born accursed. When she came out of her mother, she was not able to walk. She remains crippled but has such a good heart. Unfortunately, nobody wants to accept a disabled girl into his family. Not only has this depressed her, but she is convinced she will never find love. She has accepted her fate and I see her withering and waning every day. I am afraid we might lose her. Baba, I am a man of frugal possessions, and I can only offer you the food of my home, but this old man would remain grateful to you for the rest of his days if you could help him and his accursed daughter."

"Bring your daughter to me tomorrow, and I will do what I can," the sadhu said.

The old man left nodding his head.

One by one people began lining up before Sadhu Ananda to have their palms examined and he sat underneath the banyan tree, examining each hand, and talking to each person in detail about their lives, about what was and what was to come. At one point he glanced at the crowd before him and noticed that there were quite a few women who had also come. Faces concealed behind their *ghomtas* as they stood, some with an infant held at their hip, others either with pots of water or with plates of offerings. He wondered which village they had walked down from, he wondered if anybody recognized him.

The next morning, the old man was back with his daughter, who placed a mat next to him. Ananda poured over his chart. With brows furrowed in concentration, he made calculations in his mind, mumbling and plotting diagrams on a spare piece of paper while the village folk looked on in silence. He then looked up at the girl and asked to see both her hands.

Caressing his beard, Ananda said, "The dreaded *Rahu* and *Ketu*, the rogue planets, have teamed up and obscured her *mangala*, and that is the reason for her suffering. You must offer prayers to the *Sun God* and *Lord Indra* every day and every night for the next one month and she herself will turn her fate around."

With moist eyes, the old man joined his trembling hands in a show of respect and then placed a plateful of boiled potatoes before Ananda as he proceeded to leave.

Ananda looked at the girl and said, "Two things, dear. First, love knocks on everyone's door. It will knock on yours, too. Be alert enough to run up and receive it when you hear the knock, or it may be gone forever. Second, don't let life slip away while you wait for love, live, dear one, live for yourself!"

Quite inexplicably, a tinge of pain shot through Ananda's heart and he again looked out at the crowd that had gathered before him. His love wasn't among them.

All those years ago, he hadn't given Binodini the chance to plead with him before he left. He had left at the crack of dawn--now more than twenty years ago—never to return. He had walked towards the door one last time and then paused and turned around to take one last look at her, fast asleep, to tell her how beautiful he thought she was, to tell her how sorry he was to leave, to tell her how cruel a human being he had thought himself to be, to leave a young bride all alone in this world and go seek God in the mountains. She wouldn't understand the visions he was seeing, his inner voice that kept goading him to go to the mountains and live the life of a monk there, to starve himself, strip himself of all worldly adornments, burn in the sun, freeze in the snow, soak in the rain and pray, assume the name, Ananda and seek the Lord Almighty with all his soul. It had to be done, he had to go. And so, he left.

But he was back now, even though he thought he would never return. After all these years, his wealth consisted only of the realization that God, whoever He was, wherever He came from, did not live in the mountains. And he desired atonement. A sense of remorse stole into his heart and pierced it like a dagger.

Days turned to weeks and Sadhu Ananda became a regular sight at the *ghats* of the Sarayu, sitting underneath the shades of the great banyan, studying people's palms, telling them whether they should elect a certain *panchayat*, sow a certain kind of crop, or what turn the weather would take in the months to come. On his part, Ananda remained faithful to his task, it earned him his daily meals and a little money for his other needs. However, he always kept an eye on the womenfolk that had begun to appear, now in throngs to see him, to see if she was among them. Was she still alive? Did she still live in the same village? Did she remarry? He didn't know and fate, quite understandably didn't seem too inclined to let him know either. And he hadn't the courage to go seek her.

"So, is this what you've decided for yourself, Bino? Is this how you plan on living out your days, as the temple cook?"

Asha looked at Binodini as she smeared cooking oil on a frying pan. Bino, for her part, turned around to look at her friend and then quietly went back to what she was doing.

Asha persisted, "Bino, you aren't that old. You can still go back to your hometown and live there. You have languished in this village for twenty years, and we can tell that you don't like it here anymore than you did back in the day."

"This is my home, Asha. And why are you bringing this up suddenly, after all these years?" "Because, I can see that you are suffering, I have seen you suffer every day since that heartless madman left you. I know what you've been through, and I think you should spend your remaining days back in your hometown among your own people."

Binodini turned to look at her friend. "Asha, why are you talking like a child? You are my oldest friend and you know how my people married me off when I was all but fifteen. What makes you think they'll take me back after all these years? How do you think they'll react when suddenly appear and tell them that my husband ran away twenty years ago and that I have been living here, all alone, childless, cooking at this temple for my livelihood? Don't act like you don't know how people look upon a lone woman. This village became my home twenty years ago and will remain so."

Asha realized that in her concern for her friend and in her passion, she had wandered into a dark corner of Binodini's mind that she was secretive and fiercely protective about. But all the same, she wanted Bino to seek a new life now, enough of cooking for the village temple. After all, she was only thirty-five and could still remarry, start a new life. She decided to take another route.

"Let it go, I am sorry if I annoyed you. I am just worried about you."

"Don't worry Asha. I am okay.

"By the way, I told you about the new Sadhu that everybody is talking about, didn't I? The one who sits near the Sarayu ghat?"

"I don't remember."

"How could you forget, remember Sita was saying that everybody in the village has had their palms read by him and say that his predictions are so accurate?"

"Oh, that Sadhu! Yes, I remember Sita saying that, but I am not too keen to have my own palm read. There's nothing new he can tell me. My fate is my curse!"

"Don't you talk like that, Bino, what would you lose

just going and seeing him, who knows what your future holds?"

"I just don't want to, Asha, don't force me. These twenty years have rolled by without anything unusual, and I am happy this way. I don't want to look ahead."

"What if I said that I want to go, and want you to tag along with me to keep me company?"

"Asha, for once and for all, it's never going to happen. I don't believe in astrology and for all you know he's a crook, here to make a fool of people—like the madman I married."

One evening, as the waning sun began its descent into the horizon, Ananda, decided to head back towards his place of rest. It was a long walk back. He had come out on a stroll that afternoon by the banks of the river and had wandered off far into the forested area that lay on the farthest end of the river. It had almost been a month since he had first set foot in the village and he, being tired and resigned, was now beginning to contemplate moving on.

It was getting dark and he walked along a shallow bank where people normally bathed, filled their water-containers and lingered to chat. There was no one there today. As Ananda approached a flight of stairs leading down to the water, his eyes caught a figure down at the lowest landing, bent over the water, filling up a brass water pot. Ananda was concerned as it was dark, and the person stood the risk of slipping and falling into the water.

"You shouldn't be here at the riverbank alone this late in the evening, stranger," he called out. "All nightly creatures come out at this hour for their prey, including rogues and thieves and you may slip into the water."

The figure took its time with the filling and then slowly, holding the vessel to its hip began climbing up the stairs. Ananda could tell it was a woman. When she reached where he stood, she said, "Thank you but I can take care of myself. I needed the water. The way from the *ghat* is familiar to me, and I won't get lost. You, I can tell, are of advanced years, you should be more concerned about getting home, where do you live?"

A gentle breeze removed the clouds that covered the moon and soon the *ghat* where they stood, was bathed in moonlight and for the first time in twenty years Ananda stared into the face of Binodini.

For a moment, he was dumbstruck. In anguish, Ananda's knees weakened, and he stumbled a little. There she was, his Binodini, standing right before him. He wanted to finally let loose all his restraints and hold her, tell her that he was her Ananda and that he was back for her. Binodini, on her part, could immediately tell that the sage who stood before her was the *Sadhu baba* everybody in the village was talking about. She immediately put down her vessel, wiped her hands and folded them saying, *Namaste Baba!*

Alas! She had failed to recognize him and Ananda, still entranced, could only elicit a whimper in response. Deep down inside him, there raged a battle. His almost uncontrollable urge to reveal himself to her fought against the strictures of his rigid ascetic life that had for so long thwarted his emotions, pressing him to overcome this onrush of love. Slowly, he made a gesture of blessing.

"Baba, don't you live under the banyan tree? Come, I know the way. I'll take you there." Binodini lead Ananda in the direction of the tree and he silently followed.

Upon reaching their destination, Ananda finally managed to speak. "I am grateful to you, and you are very kind. What is your name? Tell me about your family."

"My name is Binodini, and I am alone in this world. I don't have a family."

Ananda's heart twisted in a knot and he choked. Fighting hard to control the upsurge of love inside him, he said, "Binodini, nobody is alone in this world. The Almighty is the friend and family of those who call themselves alone."

"It is the Almighty, Baba, who is the cause of my burnt luck, my ill fate."

"Never blame the Almighty, Binodini. He does all things for a reason. He guides for a reason, He leads astray for a reason. Whatever is the cause of your misery, also has a reason and a solution."

It was not Ananda's words that struck Binodini; it was his voice. Although deep and calm, it had a soothing quality to it that was not alien to her. Somewhere in the deep recesses of her heart, she felt she knew that voice, a long-forgotten voice that echoed in the empty halls of her memory.

"Baba, she said, it's getting late, and I need to return to my dwelling." She folded her hands, picked up the vessel and holding it to her hip proceeded to walk down the pathway that led away from the tree.

"Binodini, before you leave," Ananda walked towards her, "I am a saint who has come here from afar and I have taken refuge here, I repay my gratitude to the good people of this village by reading their palms and telling them their futures. People come from distant villages to see me each day, why don't you come tomorrow? I'd like to read your palm for you."

Despite her deep pessimism, Binodini, oddly, didn't feel like turning down the offer, the old man seemed sincere and pious. But she had never put much faith in astrology or any such craft that had promised a glimpse into the future. She knew what the future held for her. Her fate was sealed. She was a reject, a pariah, a lone woman in a society that viewed her kind as belonging to a man or to a family. A single woman her age, was an unwelcome oddity, a reservoir of evil and a center of unwanted attention.

"I will think about it," she said and continued her walk home.

Early the next morning, Ananda was up earlier than usual. He hurried through his morning rituals and was at his place under the tree early, meditating. As the day wore on, people began to trickle in and Ananda read their palms and gave out astrology readings, a little restlessly. Clearly distracted, he kept a watch on the paths that lead to the tree, growing a little more impatient with every passing hour.

Around late afternoon, as he was saying goodbye to the last of his visitors, he noticed a woman approaching. Her head covered in her *ghomta*, as she carried in her hand a plate of bananas. She had come.

"I was expecting you," he said. She quietly sat before him and removed her head cover. Ananda's heart swelled with affection as he glanced at her face in full light for the first time after so many years. The years hadn't taken a toll on her face and she retained the beauty that he had once closed the door to. Her lips remained full and her hair still cascaded down to her chest like they used to, two decades ago. Yet, what was not lost on him was her eyes. It was her eyes, where the humiliation, shame, anger, resentfulness and loneliness of twenty whole years had settled. And suddenly, he couldn't look at them anymore. He discovered that he was far less capable of dealing with guilt now than he used to be twenty years ago.

"Let me see your hands," he said to her gently.

Setting the plate of bananas aside, she laid both her hands out before him and for a moment their eyes met. Ananda held his gaze, but she looked away. A frisson passed through him as he took her hands in his, his mind, as if on cue flashed a panorama of scenes before his eyes—him placing a garland around her neck on their wedding day, applying vermilion on her forehead, the first time he had held her hands, him looking away when she tried to stare into his eyes, him pulling away when she drew close to him at night, him mumbling his shlokas when she was talking to him. He brushed his thoughts aside and fought hard to concentrate.

Binodini, on her part, felt nothing as her skin brushed against his. It was his gaze though, that struck her as odd and imprinted itself on her mind. She felt a vague familiarity with those eyes, they seemed to give off a quality of detachedness that she felt she had somehow crossed paths at a juncture of her life she couldn't quite place a finger on. And his voice together with every syllable that left Ananda's lips, an ineffable reaction was set off inside her. She detected an old, frayed connection with it, but couldn't tell for sure where she might have encountered it before. As she sat there under the hot afternoon sun before the ascetic who now hunched before her, pouring over her palms, she regretted her decision to have come. The few last visitors lingered and watched.

"I can detect depressions on the mounds of *Jupiter* and *Saturn* in your hands."

"What does that mean, Baba?"

Pointing at her hands he said, "these mounds that you see, these prominent mounds on the base of your fingers represent *Jupiter* and *Saturn*, planets that signify success in life, prosperity and happiness. A depressed mound means that a certain misfortune had once struck you in the prime of your life, for which you blamed yourself and for which you still are suffering."

This stunned Binodini. Slowly looking up at Ananda she said, "is that what my lines say?"

"Yes, that's what they say."

Something stirred inside her. She pressed on, "What else can you see?" Ananda returned to her palms and after a few minutes said, "Someone close to you left you. It was a man, wasn't it?"

And old, forgotten ache arose within Binodini's chest and she looked away towards the river and the adjacent banks. Twilight would be setting in, in about an hour's time and village folk could be seen heading back towards their homes, workers at temples labored, cleaning prayer paraphernalia for the evening *aarti* and *bhajan*.

Binodini's reaction wasn't lost on Ananda, who, sensing the subtle change in her demeanor, continued; "I see a well-defined break on one of the lines on your palm which signify marriage, it was your husband that left you, Binodini, wasn't it? A long time ago and you ... you still aren't over him! But is it an all-nourishing, ever forgiving, dew drop of love that you still protect in your heart or is it the hellfire of hate that burns inside you for him? That is what I am unable to see, Binodini."

A flock of birds took flight from a nearby tree in a cacophony of rustles and flaps and momentarily distracted Binodini from her gaze. She tried to speak but couldn't find her voice.

"Isn't it amazing that every little detail of our destiny is written on those lines in our hands?" Tears filled her eyes.

Ananda nodded.

"These lines are but mere maps, Binodini, they serve no purpose but to show us what was and what can be. He is alive and he still loves you."

This was about all Binodini could withstand. She immediately withdrew her hand from Ananda's and shielding her face with her veil hurried past the tree and down the lane where she had come.

Evening had come and Ananda was alone under the banyan. The day's offerings lay strewn about him. A warm wetness began to spread, down over his cheeks and into his moustache and beard. He wiped off his tears and stared across the Sarayu. The setting sun cast a golden glitter over the ripples that came cascading to the shores and the skies glowed with an orange hue. A gentle breeze blew in from the river, rustling the banyan's leaves and Ananda closed his eyes feeling caressed, comforted. He felt that the Sarayu was beginning to see his predicament and empathize with him, gently caressing the burn that raged inside him for twenty whole years. He knew that his pain was but insignificant in comparison to what he had inflicted upon Binodini even in his absence, year after year and he realized that Binodini might never accept him, never take him back. But he felt that seeing her face that day, her gentle gait, her long forefingers holding the end part of the sari, her eyes upon his, was all that his soul needed. He felt that, that was all *karma* would allow him to have, that there was no atonement for what he had brought upon her.

Ananda was lost in deep meditation early next morning when a strange restlessness took him, and he opened his eyes. She sat before him, her veil drawn over her face, with a plateful of freshly cut fruits in her hands. She had come with the earliest of his visitors and had sat patiently before him the entire time while he meditated. He smiled and said, "I enjoyed the fruits you brought yesterday, thank you."

She nodded and said, "I have brought a variety today, last night I realized that you may get tired of eating a whole dozen of bananas."

Ananda laughed in amusement. "So, she did spare me a thought last night after she went back," he thought.

"Tell me more," she said. "I want to know, what else you know about me."

He detected a tone of suppressed desperation in her voice. "Are you sure Binodini, that you can handle it?"

"Yes Baba, don't withhold anything from me. I beg you!"

"Before I begin, I want you to be courageous and believe in yourself. Trials in life will always exist, you must stay strong."

"Yes, Baba I understand. Please begin."

The few villagers that had collected around Ananda heard what had transpired between them and turned to leave, grumbling to themselves and knowing they weren't getting a *darshan* anytime soon that day.

As Binodini offered him her hands, he held them open before him and stared at her palms. How could he tell her that he didn't need to look at the lines on her hands to study her past? How could he tell her that holding her hands was the only thing that he longed for? How could he tell her that he had still loved her?

"You were a *Brahmin* girl, but very poor. And your father was the village priest, am I not right?"

"Yes, that's true. My father used to perform different *pujas* for the villagers."

"Is it true that on a visit to a certain *Brahmin*'s family, your father had met the *Brahmin*'s youngest son, and being enchanted by the boy's intelligence and profound knowledge of the *Bhagvadgita*, had decided to marry you off to him."

Binodini gaped in bewilderment. Never had she expected a sage to be so powerful as to be able to see her past in such vivid detail.

"The young man would recite stanzas from the *Gita* and his voice was smooth and melodious. Your father started to believe that the Divine resided in him. He even regarded him as *Lord Krishna's* avatar," he continued. "Within weeks, wedding plans were fixed and you, a young fifteen-year-old, who hadn't even met your husband before, saw him for the very first time on your own wedding day."

"And I had thought, that my life with Satya would be the beginning of a different existence, a happy one," Binodini said. "Different, it did turn out, but not happy! He destroyed me, Baba."

Hearing his erstwhile name from her lips shook him and he felt his restrain weaken. Despite his years of learning the holy books and his mastery of the Hindu scriptures, he began to feel a little resentful towards life. Wasn't it God who had trapped both him and Binodini in His strange machinations? Wasn't it Him that had taken residence in his mind when he was but a boy, begun appearing in his dreams by the time he was a teenager, asking him to detach himself from family, take up the robes and seek Him? And wasn't it Him who, having uprooted Satya from his marital home had transformed him to Sadhu Ananda and had ultimately refused to reveal Himself to him? What this His grand plan?

"Binodini, listen to me carefully; I have faced great disappointments in life too. My one desire in this world was to do my faithful service to God, to seek Him, love Him more than anything else in this world and live my days serving Him. But I realized that my way was wrong. He had planned something else for me entirely and I misread His directions. I made a mistake, but I believe that I deserve atonement. Would you forgive your husband Binodini, ever?"

Binodini, who had trailed off, turned her gaze at Ananda now and looked straight into his eyes. A tear flowed out of one of her eyes and rolled down her face; "After putting me through all this for twenty years, Baba? Knowing what society does to a single woman whose husband's whereabouts nobody knows?"

She withdrew her hands from Ananda's and began to get up rather resolutely. Ananda's heart sensed the ominous and with great effort, he contained himself.

"Binodini, people are often led astray by powers beyond their understanding, it doesn't mean that they completely forget their familial ties, the bindings of their hearts!"

Binodini, who had begun walking down the path back to the village, turned around to look at him and said, "That may be so, but the damage that they leave in their wake is irreparable, unpardonable. Baba, a relationship doesn't involve only one person, it takes two! I can never forgive him, and I will never take him back, neither in this lifetime nor in any of the rest!"

The rising sun created a bright arch over the Sarayu's surface and life at the *ghat*, early the next day, had just begun showing signs of coming out of its reverie. A rooster nearby heralded the morning with its call and almost immediately, as if on cue, a whole flock of pigeons fled from a nearby temple roof in a raucous clatter. The small villages, their many temples, the steps that lead down to the water, the many beggars, the flower and fruit vendors, the village folk, some taking their first dips in the river, others setting up shop in the bazaars nearby—all the elements of the immense microcosm that existed around the great river, their mother, the Sarayu, were set into motion by the rising sun. There were anxious devotees in the temples to receive the blessings that the river Sarayu was capable of according. To these village folks, if the Sarayu was their mother, it was the sun that was their father.

An old man came to the banyan tree and not finding the Sadhu there, sat down to wipe his forehead. Soon others from neighboring villages started populating the space around the tree and not finding Ananda, decided to wait. Some squatted and lit their pipes, while others set up a hushed murmur. Soon platefuls of offerings began collecting on the platform where Ananda usually sat, but there was no sign of him. As the day wore on, the gathering began to thin, and the murmur gave way to a noisy clamor. People went back the way they came, some wondered where Ananda had gone off to while others felt certain he was gone for good. The old man sat at the same place gazing intently at the spot that Ananda used to occupy. By late afternoon, when Ananda hadn't returned still, it began to become clear to the village folk that perhaps the mystical sage, the powerful Sadhu Ananda had after all abandoned them and moved on in his higher quest, to some other blessed land. Some felt angered by such a sudden, unannounced departure while others simply shrugged and walked off. But the old man remained, his eyes, fixed on Ananda's seat. A man came up to him and said, "It looks like the Sadhu Baba isn't coming back today, so you might as well return home and come back tomorrow again. Have you come from afar?"

"I cannot leave without kissing the feet of the man who saved my daughter." The man stood looking at him inquiringly.

"The Baba's advice to my daughter, together with our prayers in strict accordance with his instructions, has paid off. The deformity of her leg is slowly going away, she may soon walk normally."

The news of Ananda's disappearance spread fast. Village folk speculated about the reasons of his sudden exit. Tales ranged from the plausible to the bizarre. Some said the Sadhu had been quietly smuggled off to another town by some wealthy *zamindar* to help him steer his fortunes from doom while others said assuredly that they had seen him, suddenly at the dead of the night, levitate to the skies and then take flight.

The news finally reached Binodini, who had avoided going to the *ghat* since her last meeting with Ananda. Asha, who met Binodini in the marketplace, said, "Bino, remember that Sadhu I was talking to you about the other day?"

Careful not to betray any emotion, the mention of Ananda might bring out in her, she continued on her path, looking ahead.

"Yes, I do, what happened to him?"

"He disappeared a couple of days back. Just disappeared in thin air. No one knows where he went."

Binodini smirked. "What did I tell you on the first day? Didn't I tell you that he was a crook? Now look, he has done exactly as I predicted, he has run off after feeding people gibberish about their futures and taking favors in return."

"Bino, I heard great things about the man's ability, he must have had his reasons, some sort of compulsion for leaving".

Binodini said no more. Face down, she silently made her way down the dusty path. About a mile ahead, the path forked into two with one dusty road leading to the village market and the second, to the *ghat*. At the point where the road split, Binodini paused and then took the latter.

The patch of ground where the banyan stood, was desolate and devoid of life, save for a handful of crows that jumped among the plates of offerings tentatively, pecking and devouring the sundry flowers and fruits that Ananda had left behind. Rubbish lay strewn where the village people would congregate. Ananda's seat at the raised platform at the base of the banyan, which, till a few days back was abuzz with village folk and their clamor, lay bare. A breeze blew Binodini's hair as she stood before the tree. For a moment, she wanted to sit down and wait. Perhaps Ananda really had wandered off somewhere nearby and would, by dint of some coincidence, turn up and would find her there, perhaps he had, by virtue of his powers passed into an unknown oblivion only to appear if she came—she would never know.

Halfway on her way back home, she said to herself, "I told her, I told her he was nothing but a crook, I told her that he, too, would leave!"

In all her vulnerability, she moaned and cried for his coming, she knew that he had come back into her real life. In awakening and regaining strength, she realized it was all a dream.

The months began to pass and soon the skies grew dark with heavy, nimbus clouds flashing and rumbling. The first winds rushed through the village, blowing and surging their way through the trees and homes, removing roofs from the tops of huts and sending people scurrying for cover. Despite the terrors of a storm or the likelihood of a flood, many a face in the village bore a silent smile. As the winds picked up pace and the sun concealed itself behind a thick blanket of rain clouds, the temple bells along the *ghats* of the Sarayu came to life, all at once, tinkling and chiming for the propitiation of *Lord Indra*, the air was pierced by the sound of conch shells, emanating from homes across the river banks and the great river itself licked and caressed the foot of the banks mischievously.

Ananda, the great Sage, with time, had receded to the back alleys of people's memories.

His seat at the banyan tree, lay unoccupied.

Binodini stepped out of her home into her porch that afternoon and looked up at the sky. It wasn't bright, but all the sudden the air was unusually calm. No chirping could be heard from the trees and immediate heavy rainfall seemed unlikely. The pots and pitchers at her home were empty and the last cupful of water had been consumed that morning. Despite the calm outside she felt a slight tremor in her chest, a hint of trepidation. But water was needed, nonetheless.

Even the temple where she worked was a mile and a half away, too long a walk in the rain to soothe a parched throat. She lit a lamp before the deity at home and prayed. Then, holding the pitcher to her hip, she set out towards the river to fetch water. She wanted to get her pitcher filled up before hurrying back home. As she set out, she realized that the faint tremor in her heart hadn't gone. She wondered if she was falling ill, she had been feeling this way for a few days now and had not attached much importance to it but that afternoon, she felt concerned. As her feet touched the soft, moist ground, her mind wandered to Ananda. A smile crossed her face and she continued on her way to the Sarayu.

The banks of the river had just begun to come into view, when the winds picked up pace. The insidious silence in the air was now slowly replaced by a strong gust of wind carrying the smell of rain across the *ghat*, waving the trees and rustling the leaves and almost immediately, darkness began setting in. Binodini quickened her pace. The winds set up a whistle now and a quick blue crack appeared overhead, ripping the sky apart and almost immediately a suppressed rumble sounded, echoing across the river and its banks. Binodini hurriedly held on to the end of her *sari*, that had now started to billow in the wind. She had been caught in a storm before but never had her heart beat so wildly. A cold hand seemed to rise from the pit of her stomach and seize her throat. The temples on one of the banks began sounding its bells and soon little lamps began to appear in windows and conch shells were heard over the lapping sound of the waters of the Sarayu. The whip-like winds made it impossible for Binodini to walk any faster, yet she trudged on gripping the pitcher tight, laboring against the winds that swayed her from one side to another. The storm had escalated quickly. The lightning forks flashing with zigzag outlines lit up the whole area, the first drop of rain fell on her face. Suddenly, the rain came down in torrents followed by another blinding flash.

By the time she reached the steps that led down to the water, random and sudden gusts of wind had wreaked chaos on the *ghat*, and she barely managed to stand upright. Her vision was almost entirely blurred, and she was soaked. Shivering in the cold rain, she decided that there was no going back now. She had come all the way to the river and would not go back without a full pitcher. A gust of wind blew into her face bringing with it, dirt and leaves and her pitcher dropped from her hands. Blinded by the dirt, Binodini struggled to grab the end of her *sari* to wipe off her face when a strong gush of wind knocked her off her feet. She fell on her side right on the edge of the footsteps and began tumbling down the steps. She flailed her arms about violently to hold on to something but the winds, the dirt and the darkness had completely blocked out her vision. Oddly, during her fall, she thought she heard someone calling out her name from afar. When her head hit one of the last steps down near the water, and in a moment of visibility, Binodini witnessed the wrath of the Sarayu. No more was the Sarayu, the life-giving mother that had kept the civilization on her banks alive with her water, it had now assumed the avatar of the *Goddess Kali*, the warrior, the slayer, the destroyer, the restorer of the balance between good and evil. As Binodini bounced off the last steps of the *ghat*, the stormy waves that crashed against them accepted her within their fold rather gently. Arms flailing, her legs struggled to find ground but the final piece of hard land that her feet touched, was slippery and it smoothly passed her into the water. Struggling to keep her head from submerging, she gasped for breath, wide eyed with terror. As the Sarayu began pulling Binodini towards her bosom, she began to let go of the struggle. Just before she went down, she had a brief glimpse of her parents and Satya standing at the banks, calmly smiling at her, holding out their arms, beckoning her and welcoming her to be among them. Water rushed into her mouth and then, darkness. And eternity.

She rose into the air, above the choppy waters as the raindrops pricked her face. Lying suspended, she glided up the steps wherefrom she had tumbled and flew onto the landing. She felt water pouring out of her mouth and nose. Gently, she landed on a surface and her face was wiped dry. Her *sari* that had come undone was draped across her chest. Far across the expanses of her mind she heard an echo. A familiar voice calling out her name, *Bino, Bino!*

She wanted to answer but felt choked. The call continued, *Bino! Bino!* She tried harder to call out in response, but her throat appeared to be full of water and she gurgled, choking. The call came again, now closer, much closer, *Bino! Binodini, open your eyes!* followed by vigorous shaking and thumps on her back. She recognized the voice now. It was Satya's voice. Satya had come to receive her. She made a desperate effort to open her eyes and suddenly, with a violent cough, she regurgitated water and a pair of hands sat her up. She was back at the *ghat*. Looking around she realized that she was underneath the banyan tree and felt a pair of powerful hands holding her upright.

"Bino, can you see me?"

Trembling and breathing hard, she turned her gaze towards the source of the voice and recognized who it was that spoke to her. Soaked completely in his ochre robe, that stuck to his body, sat Ananda—her Satya—folding her to his heart. And then they looked at each other's eyes, and love shone through their tears.

"I saw you tumble down into the water, Bino," he said. "I kept calling out your name, but the winds carried my voice with them."

A smile illuminated her pale face. It was getting harder for her to breathe, and she opened her mouth to speak but all she could produce was a wheeze. The water had reached her lungs. She held his arm tight in an effort to speak and Ananda grimaced at the pressure of her hands as he felt her agony. With great effort she said, "Why did you leave me, Satya?"

The floodgates inside Ananda that he had held together

for twenty years finally broke and his head hung low as he shook and wept, his face screwed up in the rainwater and tears that swirled down his face into his beard.

"It has been so long," she said. "Did you find Him?" She took one last breath as her head fell into Ananda's lap.

There was a lull in the rain and the sky cleared. It was a day as bright as any and the birds chirped merrily from their nests up in the trees. It was like spring and soft green grass, mottled by tiny flowers of different colors, carpeted the grounds on which she lay. The cool shade of the banyan tree swayed with drops of rain trickling down its leaves. The River Sarayu was calm again and resplendent, sparkling like a bed of a thousand lilting diamonds on its surface as a ray of sun broke through the clouds. Ananda and Bino's hands remained joined and for the first time after, after twenty years, her Satya looked down lovingly at her eyes. There was no sorrow on her face; it was a loving and quiet face, like one who had waited patiently through all the years. She had waited for him, watched for him.

"Yes, my Bino, I finally found Him. He was with you. I wandered in distant lands carrying a heavy burden of sorrow, at last, coming to you I have surrendered myself at your feet. Won't you kindly wash away my endless afflictions with the waters of your love."

It was not long before the villagers gathered under the old banyan tree on the banks of River Sarayu. It was a mournful sight. The men were downcast and sullen while all the women wailed. And standing among them, was the old man and his daughter who was no longer crippled, cured by the sadhu, both wiping tears away from their furrowed faces.

GLOSSARY

- *aarti* – A Hindu ritual of worship in which a light (usually from a flame of a candle) is offered to one or more deities. It also refers to the songs in praise of a deity.
- *ashrams* – A religious home for a sage or Hindu monastery.
- *avatar* – Human manifestation of a Hindu god that would appear on Earth.
- *baba* – Father, or referring to Father out of respect to a sage or wise one.
- *Benares* – City located in India on the banks of the river Ganges, referred to a sacred city for pilgrimage.
- *bhajan* – A religious song.
- *bhikharini* – A woman beggar.
- *biryani* – An Indian cuisine made with spiced rice and meat, fish, or vegetables.
- *boti* – A long blade that is attached to a block of wood where the person uses his foot to hold down the block

of wood and grate foods like coconut, pumpkin, vegetables, or meat.

- *Brahmin* – A priest or teacher and a member of the highest caste order.
- *chapatis* – Unleavened flatbread.
- *chital* – Species of knifefish, also known as *chitala chitala.*
- *chula* – Oven or earthen stove.
- *Chup!* – Be quiet! Shut up!
- *curry* – An Indian dish, usually sauce based with meat or vegetables.
- *dalit* – Outcast, a member of the lowest caste.
- *darshan* – A chance to view or see a holy person, a saint, or deity.
- *darzi* – A tailor.
- *dhobani* – Woman who washes clothes; washerwoman.
- *dhobi* – Man who washes clothes; washerman.
- *Didi*– Older sister; term used to address an older sister.
- *diya* – An oil lamp usually small made of clay, ghee, and cotton.
- *dora* – Stripe; long line or mark.
- *Durga (Goddess)* – One of the principal Goddesses in Hindu mythology, meaning "invincible" who was known to have killed a buffalo demon, and celebrated traditionally in a large festival period in the fall.

- *Ekadashi* - Eleventh day of the lunar month; considered a spiritual day and often observed by fasting for the entire day.
- *Gayatri mantra* - A popular sacred hymn dedicated to the sun deity.
- *ghat/Dobhi Ghat* - A series of steps that lead down to a river. Dhobi Ghat is referred to the world's largest *ghat* used to wash clothes by the river, found in Mumbai.
- *ghomta* - The loose end of the sari that is pulled over the head and face as a veil.
- *ghungroo* - Ankle bells used in classical Indian folk dances, such as *Kathak dance*.
- *Gita/Bhagvadgita* - A sacred book, considered as the "Bible" in Hindu scripture, which was composed about 200 BC, containing the discussion between Lord Krishna and the Indian hero Arjuna on human nature and the purpose of life.
- *harmonium* - A keyboard instrument in which music is created by a hand-operated   bellow to drive air into metal reeds, similar to an accordion.
- *Indra (God)* - Hindu counter part of Greek God Zeus, the God of the sky and thunder. He also wields the lightening thunderbolt.
- *jhol* - Sauce or gravy left in a vegetable or meat dish.

- *Kathak dance* - A classical Northern Indian dance during which the dancer is able to tell
- stories through facial expressions, intricate hand movements, and repetitive foot movements.
- *Kayastha* - Middle class caste, typically merchants or local businessmen.
- *kirana* - Small grocery store.
- *Lakshmi (Goddess)* - Goddess of wealth and fortune; wife to *Lord Vishnu.*
- *lungi* - A garment worn by men, similar to a sarong, wrapped around the waist and extending to the ankles.
- *Mahabharata* - A Sanskrit epic, describing a civil war between the Pandavas and the Kauravas in the kingdom of Kurukshetra about the 9th century BC, resulting in the text of the Bhagavad-Gita.
- *mala* - A bead or a set of beads commonly used to keep count while reciting or chanting a prayer.
- *Mangala* - Name for the planet Mars and worshiped as the God of War.
- *mantra* - A sacred hymn.
- *Mashi* - Aunt.
- *Memsaab* - Title for a woman in a position of authority.
- *moksha* - Release from the cycle of rebirth impelled by the law of karma.

- *Ojhas* – Non-traditional doctors or healers who used natural/supernatural powers to help heal.
- *paan* – A betel leaf with areca nut often mixed with tobacco, widely used as a stimulant. Often chewed and spat, it leaves teeth stained dark yellow/orange.
- *panchayat* – Village council.
- *pabda* – Species of fish found in Asian countries.
- *pipal* – A fig tree, regarded as sacred by Buddhists.
- *Pishima* – Father's sister.
- *pujo/puja* – An act of worship and prayer.
- *pungi* – Type of flute, commonly played by snake charmers.
- *rajbhog* – Popular Bengali sweet, made from cottage cheese, saffron, and syrup.
- *Rabindra sangeet* – Songs written and composed by poet laureate, *Rabindranath Tagore.*
- *Ramayana* – A Sanskrit epic, telling the story of the banishment of Rama from his kingdom, the abduction of his wife Sita by a demon and her rescue, and Rama's eventual restoration to the throne.
- *rohu* – Species of carp found in Asian countries, also called *rui*.
- *rotis* – Flat round bread.
- *sadhu* – A saint; holy man.
- *sandesh* – A type of Bengali dessert, made with cooked

and dried milk and sugar, formed into numerous shapes and sizes.

- *sari* – A traditional woman's garment made a single drape of cloth typically wrapped around the waist and one end draped over the shoulder.
- *surya pranam* – A prayer dedicated and honoring the sun; sun salutations.
- *teen patti* – Popular gambling card game, similar to Poker, also called *flush.*
- *tilak* – A mark worn by a Hindu on the forehead to indicate caste, status, or sect.
- *tolas* – A old unit of weight used in South Asia, equal to ~11.34 grams.

ACKNOWLEDGMENTS

HAVING THE IDEA of writing a book and turning it into a physical entity does not come without hardship and tremendous support. The experience is both challenging and rewarding and I especially want to thank and pay tribute to several individuals that helped make this happen. To Brenda Bradshaw, I owe it all. She let me in to the thick and impenetrable fortress of the publishing world with no second thoughts or qualms whatsoever. "These stories are wonderful, are you sure you want to publish with us?" That's all she could say. It was taken up further by two other remarkable ladies from Amphorae Publishing. Special thank you to Kristina Makansi, my patient editor, who spent countless hours trying to decipher the Indian words that were foreign to her and Lisa Miller who was there to satisfy all my naive questions as a novice writer.

Going back a bit further to the days when my rough drafts were incredibly rough, I want to thank my friend Jona Ghosh, a creative writer and teacher herself, for suggestions and thoughtful critique. My wonderful nephew, Ronojoy Basu, who is a prolific reader and writer himself, who I would exchange sweets for reading my stories during the holiday breaks. My niece Reshmi Basu, who always encouraged me to write and continue my passion. And my trusted friend, Indrani Roy, who at the time when I first wrote these stories, was not only the first to read them, but took the time to illustrate the beautiful artwork you see throughout the book.

Finally, I would like to acknowledge the support and love of my family. They all kept me going with words of encouragement. My youngest son, Jay Sen, who guided me with rules for communicating clearly and concisely. My daughter-in-law, Ruchy Sen, who spent time reading and editing the stories, and my older sister, Anita Ghosh, who took the time to proofread my book and make sure I was making proper use of the Queen's English!

And lastly, this book wouldn't have been possible without the help of my eldest son, Shawn Sen, who spent hours helping me improve the stories to their full potential and continually pushed me to never settle for a final draft.

ABOUT THE AUTHOR

Bharati Sen originally spent much of her childhood growing up in Myanmar and West Bengal. She completed a master's degree in International Relations in India before moving to the United States. Much of her writing is inspired while living in the city of Kolkata, focusing on ordinary individuals and providing fascinating glimpses into the challenges of being a woman in India.

Her debut book, *On the Banks of River Sarayu*, is a collection of short stories detailing the lives of hidden individuals, particularly women, living in the lower strata of Indian society, describing the emotional and raging disparities that often lead to bittersweet endings. Bharati currently lives in Tulsa, Oklahoma with her husband and two sons. She is greatly involved in the Indian community and contributes to local magazines.